BRENDA JACKSON

CAPTIVATED BY LOVE

Love Passion & Promise

LOVE, PASSION AND PROMISE BOOKS
are published by

The Madaris Publishing Company
P O Box 28267
Jacksonville, FL 32226

Cover design and layout by Nuance Art, LLC
Art direction by aCreativeNuance.com

ISBN 978-0-9799165-5-7

10 9 8 7 6 5 4 3 2 1
Printed in the United States of America

Love, Passion and Promise

An Imprint of the Madaris Publishing Company

www.madarispublishing.com

Dear Readers,

I am proud to present the seventh book from the Madaris Publishing Company, **Captivated By Love.**

When I began writing the Granger Series (A Brothers Honor; A Man's Promise; and A Lover's Vow), I had no idea my readers would fall in love with Sheppard Granger, the father of the three Granger brothers. I received letters and emails from readers wanting Sheppard Granger and Carson Boyett's story. Readers mainly wanted to know how they met, how they kept their love alive during his incarceration and how they are doing since he was exonerated of killing his wife.

When I decided to honor my readers' wishes and write Sheppard's story, I knew it would be a special one. Here is a man who'd lost a lot yet kept his dignity and reached out to others with his kindness and wisdom. I knew Sheppard's story would be the perfect way to kick off the next Granger connected series adventure, The Protector Series.

The Protector Series features three of the men Sheppard mentored who eventually became bodyguards to his sons. The men were Striker Jennings, Quasar Patterson and Stonewall Courson. Book 1, Forged In Desire features Striker Jennings and will be released January 31, 2017. Book 2 features Quasar Patterson and is titled Seized By Seduction and will hit the bookstores in April. And Book 3, titled Locked in Temptation, features Stonewall Courson and will be released in July.

A listing of all my books is found on my website at
www.brendajackson.net

Happy Reading!

Brenda Jackson

ACKNOWLEDGEMENTS

To Brenda Chin, editor extraordinaire. Thanks for the wonderful editorial work that you did on this novel.

To Connie Moore and Brenda Woodbury. Thanks for such wonderful promotional campaigns for all the books in the Granger Series…especially this one.

To Gerald Jackson, Jr. and Brandon Jackson. Thanks for your love and encouragement. Your mother loves you!

To the ladies of Diva Dayz 2016. Thanks for such a great time in Key West, Florida. I felt the love and needed the fellowship.

He who finds a wife finds what is good and receives favor from the LORD.
Proverbs 18:22 NIV

IN LOVING MEMORY OF THE MAN WHO WILL
ALWAYS AND FOREVER BE THE LOVE OF MY LIFE
GERALD JACKSON, SR.

FEBRUARY 11, 1951 – DECEMBER 15, 2013

THE GRANGER SERIES BOOKS BY BRENDA JACKSON

A Brother's Honor
A Man's Promise
A Lover's Vow
Captivated by Love

THE PROTECTOR SERIES BOOKS BY BRENDA JACKSON

Forged in Desire
Seized by Seduction
Locked in Temptation

PROLOGUE

Determined not to awaken his wife, Sheppard Granger eased out of bed and walked over to the huge bay window. There was a crescent moon in the velvety sky, and what seemed like a million twinkling stars served as a panoramic backdrop.

It was a beautiful night in December, three weeks before Christmas. Decorations were up and from where Sheppard stood, he could see that someone had strung colorful lights along the entrance to his family's estate, Sutton Hills, and several of the trees in the yard displayed numerous colorful lights as well. The horses had been stabled for the night and the high pitched roof of the equestrian center was barely visible in the darkness. In a few days, Christmas lights would likely find their way there as well, he figured.

Forecasters predicted that the residents of Charlottesville could be in for their first snowfall of the winter season this weekend, with the cold weather remaining through the holidays. All he had to do was take note of the frost on the outside of the window to conclude the forecasters were probably right. But he could handle snowfall or whatever the weather produced. He was just glad to finally be home. This was the house he had grown up in. The main house. His parents' home. And it was the one he had decided to move into instead of the one he'd shared with his first wife.

Standing there, he recalled the years he was locked up, not able to look out a window to see the moon or stars and definitely not a bunch of Christmas lights. At times, it had been impossible to determine when day turned into night or night into day. For years, he hadn't seen snowfall or rain, and had missed the feel of wind beating against his face. He had almost forgotten the sound of birds chirping or frogs croaking; the feel of wet grass or the sight of a flower blooming.

For fifteen years, Sheppard had been a man living behind bars for a crime he hadn't committed. But that was over and he'd been exonerated of all charges. It felt good to be home at Sutton Hills. Back with his three sons and the women they'd married. He was still in awe after the birth of his first grandchild, Rylan Bradford Granger.

Sheppard wished his father could have been there for the delivery of the eight pound, three ounce healthy boy. Richard Granger would have been proud to usher in the fourth generation of Grangers. Unfortunately, a heart attack had claimed his life several months back. And as much as Sheppard wished his father hadn't died, he credited Richard's death as the spark that started the fire.

He was well aware that if his father hadn't died, there would not have been a reason for his three sons - Jace, Caden and Dalton - to return home to Charlottesville. No reason for them to make that deathbed promise to Richard to save Granger Aeronautics and do whatever it took to get Sheppard out of prison. Somehow, his sons had managed to do both, just like they'd promised the old man they would.

Promises made. Promises kept.

"Sheppard?"

He turned at the sound of the feminine voice and met the gaze of the woman he proudly called his wife. Yesterday, they had celebrated their first wedding anniversary. He'd wanted to take her out of town for a few days, however, she'd preferred a quiet dinner with just the two of them. Then they'd returned home to spend the rest of the night in bed enjoying each other.

Carson Boyett Granger was everything he'd ever wanted. More importantly, she was every single thing he needed, even when it looked like he was destined to serve thirty years in prison. The last thing he thought he'd find while locked up behind bars was the love of a lifetime. A woman who, for five years, had shown him that if you truly believed, dreams could come true.

His wife had looked exquisite tonight. The dress she'd worn had been absolutely perfect. It had been red--his favorite color--and the sleek design had skated along all her seductive curves. The side split that ran up her leg had exposed an appealing thigh. He'd noted the heads of several men turn to stare when they'd entered the restaurant.

He'd barely been able to keep his own eyes off her during dinner and scarcely recalled what had been on his plate. However, he had remembered every detail of what happened once they came back home. He had leaned against the closed bedroom door and watched her strip. His heart had pounded with every stitch she'd removed, letting each piece of clothing pool at her feet. Her dress, garter, bra, panties...

His heart was pounding now at the memory. He had met Carson about six years ago, when the family of one of the young inmates he mentored had hired her to represent their son when they pushed for a retrial. The first time he'd seen her, he had been totally and completely captivated. He'd been convinced then and was still convinced now, that she was the most beautiful woman he'd ever met.

The attraction between him and Carson had been instantaneous, although he'd fought it like hell. First off, she was nearly ten years his junior. And from what he'd heard about her, she was a top-notch attorney who frequented the prison to meet with the young inmates, pro bono.

He, on the other hand, a man accused of murdering his wife, had nothing to offer her. But Carson hadn't cared once they had been honest about their feelings. When he'd gotten dissatisfied with the way his own attorney was handling his business, he had replaced the man with Carson. It was a decision he'd never regretted.

Realizing he hadn't answered, he spoke up. "Yes, sweetheart?"

"You, okay?"

A smile touched his lips. Carson always made him her major concern. Her main priority. That was something his first wife, Sylvia, never did. "I'm fine. Just thinking."

"At three in the morning?"

He chuckled. "Yes, at three in the morning. I guess some habits are hard to break."

While in prison, he hadn't been able to sleep until he knew all the young men on his floor, most of whom he'd mentored and who'd come to be known as Shep's boys, had been accounted for and were in their cells asleep. It was only then that he could close his eyes and rest.

"Then we will think together," she said, easing out of the bed.

Sheppard drew in a deep calming breath, trying to keep his libido in check, while watching her cross the room to him. The moonlight shining through the window cast a glow on her naked body. Mesmerized, he believed she was the most desirable woman to walk the face of the earth, and he fought against the turbulent sensations fueled by intense desire from overtaking him again that night.

He was satisfied in believing…most of the time…that this continued influx of sexual need for her was due to the fact they were still making up for lost time. For so long, the very idea of making love to her was a dream and never a reality. For five years, they'd done everything but consummate their relationship and it hadn't been easy. Just looking at her made the air shimmer and could cause a tightening low in his gut.

When he opened his arms, she quickened her steps and walked right into them. He tightened his hold on her and at that moment, he needed her. Here in his arms. So many times while in prison, she'd been his lifeline. His calm after the storm. He didn't know of a more loving, dedicated and loyal individual. Carson was someone who loved deeply. She wasn't quick to make judgements. And if she claimed you as a friend, it was for life.

Sheppard inhaled her scent, a fragrance he'd come to accept as uniquely hers. Her sensuous aroma was his weakness, and usually just a whiff could bring him to his knees...and while he was down on them, he usually took the opportunity to satisfy another sense. His taste. He loved being on his knees, tasting her between those gorgeous legs. From the way she would groan, he could tell she liked it as well. As far as he was concerned, her body was a perfect match to his, and as soon as their naked flesh connected, he was always caught up in a wild rush of sensual hunger.

When she lifted her head from his chest and tilted it back to look up at him, he lowered his lips to hers, taking her mouth with a hunger that nearly overpowered him. It didn't matter that they'd made love mere hours ago and had

6

fallen asleep in each other's arms. Nor did it matter that he kissed her all the time, so there was no reason for his greed right now.

His only excuse was that Carson had the ability to make her feminine power surround him. And it didn't help matters when she began making those sinfully erotic movements with her hips…like she was doing now. It would not have been so bad if they hadn't been naked, but since they were skin-to-skin, sexual desire quickly began to curl in his stomach. How could it not when he was drowning in woman? His woman. His wife. His best friend.

And when she began returning his kiss, stroke for stroke, he knew where all this would lead again. But even when he released her mouth, he began brushing kisses against her lips, while whispering promises he intended to keep later. For now, he just needed to hold her.

"So what were you thinking about?" she asked, resting her head on his chest once more. "Do you regret having the boat- house torn down and rebuilt elsewhere?"

He shook his head. "No. That was a good decision. I don't have to see it whenever I look out this window."

The boathouse was where his first wife Sylvia had been murdered sixteen years ago. It was also the place where she would often entertain her lovers, right under her family's noses. There definitely hadn't been any shame in Sylvia Granger's game.

"Then what got you up at three in the morning?"

He drew in a deep breath, inhaling her luscious scent through his nostrils. "I'll be spending a full day at the office tomorrow."

Her eyes widened. "You will?"

"Yes." He'd dropped by Granger Aeronautics several times over the past year since his release from prison, mainly to see employees who'd been there when he had been second in command under his father. It had felt good walking through the doors and the changes in the place had amazed him. His father had worked hard to keep the company moving ahead without him. And his oldest son, Jace, was doing an excellent job in keeping it forging forward.

"I figured it was time to start getting acclimated to everything. I talked to Jace and he thinks it's a good idea to get started before the holidays. He wants to take Shana and the baby to their cabin in the mountains the first week in January."

"I think that's a great idea."

"What? You're happy that Jace, Shana and the baby are taking off to the Shenandoah Mountains for a week after the holidays?" he asked.

"That too, but I was mostly thinking about you returning to Granger Aeronautics sooner than planned. You've been free for a year and I can tell you're getting restless."

Was he? The day after he'd been released from prison, he had done the one thing he couldn't wait any longer to do--marry Carson. The wedding had been held here on Sutton Hills, with family and close friends attending, as well as many of the men he liked to think of as his "surrogate sons". Young men he'd met while confined, who had eventually gotten their freedom, as well--either by serving the time they'd been given or by getting their convictions overturned when new evidence proved their innocence.

The number of innocent men who were locked up was atrocious. That was the message he had taken to Capitol Hill two weeks ago when he'd been summoned to appear before a congressional hearing regarding the need to overhaul the criminal judicial system.

His release from prison had made international headlines, especially since the takedown of the organized crime cartel responsible for killing his wife and numerous others played a large role. Arrests were still being made and notable politicians and businessmen were among those indicted.

He had refused to do interviews with the major networks until after his honeymoon. He and Carson had deserved some privacy, so they'd taken a three week trip to Hawaii. But they had returned in time to attend his son Caden's benefit concert. Sheppard's second-born son, who'd always loved to play the saxophone, had become a Grammy-award winning musician in his absence. The concert had been sold out and it had been the first time Sheppard had seen Caden perform.

"I didn't want to rush back to Granger Aeronautics on a full-time basis too soon," he said, taking his fingers and twirling a few strands of her hair, loving the feel of the silky texture. "Jace has done an outstanding job, with Caden and Dalton helping out. Besides, there were a lot of documents I needed to read, classes I need to take to get re-certified in a number of areas before going back."

"I understand."

He held her gaze and knew she honestly did. "And what do you understand, sweetheart?"

She wrapped her arms around his neck and leaned up on her tip-toes to brush a kiss across his lips. "You like the idea of your sons taking part in the company. You said it was your father's dream, and I think, deep down, that it was your dream as well. Now it's a reality and you don't want them to feel that they aren't needed."

A smile curved Sheppard's lips. It was at times like this, he wondered how she could read him so well. And because he felt there was more, he said. "Go on."

She nodded. "Jace is a natural born leader and you know he's not going anywhere, whether you return or not. I can see him pulling up his shirt sleeves and working hard by your side. Caden loves his music and will continue to try to do both. But I think you know which of the two is his first love…besides Shiloh."

Yes, he knew. Marriage to the woman who had been his first love was good for Caden. He went into the office every day, but Sheppard wondered if Caden ever thought about returning to the concert circuit he'd given up to help his brothers save Granger Aeronautics.

"And then there's Dalton."

Sheppard chuckled and shook his head. His youngest son was...special. Marriage was definitely good for him, especially when his wife was a woman like Jules. The two of them were good together and constantly challenged each other. Sheppard was convinced that if it hadn't been for Jules, Dalton would have taken off to parts unknown, chasing behind some skirt, the moment Sheppard had walked out of prison a free man. Wanderlust had been Dalton's middle name. But still, Sheppard wasn't sure how much longer Dalton would be able to dedicate his life to Granger Aeronautics. He knew his son had used up all his vacation days--and then some he didn't really have on the books--to accompany Jules, who was a private investigator, on a couple of her business trips.

"You're ready to go back, Sheppard. Granger Aeronautics is calling your name."

"Is it?" He'd always thought so, but lately he wasn't sure. Being incarcerated for fifteen years had a way of making you take another look at your life. A lot of things that used to be important to him had become less so. He shook his head slightly. There was one thing he could say about his wife... She knew him and had an uncanny ability to read him at times.

She didn't say anything for a minute as she studied him with that intense gaze of hers. She looked closely into his eyes and he was certain she saw the love he felt for her. But with the lifting of her brow, he was sure she'd detected something else as well. "Umm, but then maybe it's not. Tell me how you feel, Sheppard."

He drew in a deep breath and then taking her hand, he led her across the room and back to bed. This would be a conversation he wanted to have while they were lying down with her body nestled next to his.

The moment they got underneath the covers, he pulled her to him, their limbs automatically entwined, her head resting against his chest. "Lately I've been thinking about not returning to Granger Aeronautics on a permanent basis."

"Why?"

He paused a moment and then said, "Dad had planned to retire before I was arrested for Sylvia's death. Once I was convicted, retirement had no longer been an option for him and he'd worked tirelessly for the next fifteen years to keep the company afloat for his grandsons."

"And for your return," she added.

"Yes, for my return. Had I come home when Dad assumed I would, I would be doing the same thing he'd been doing, right about now…thinking about retiring and leaving the company to my sons. Jace is doing a fantastic job. I don't want to get in the way. He loves GA as much as I once did."

"Once? But not now?"

"Not with the passion I use to. My heart is elsewhere, Carson."

She twisted around in his arms and met his gaze. "Where?"

"The Sheppard Granger Foundation for Troubled Teens. I'm needed more there than at GA."

Carson didn't say anything as she thought about her husband's admission. It was one only a man such as Sheppard could make. He had been locked up for fifteen years. He'd been inside the walls, had seen what prison could do to a person if they didn't have an advocate on the inside who was not afraid to fight their battles. But the foundation Sheppard had established after being released from prison took things even farther. It was created to stop at-risk teens before they could even get that far, to keep them from going to jail in the first place.

She'd known that he had been working with Reverend Luther Thomas, even from inside the walls of prison. She'd heard the story from Sheppard that Luther, a convict himself, had been released after being locked up for six years before his attorney fought for and won a new trial. New evidence was submitted that proved the DNA on the rape victim didn't belong to Luther. Even better, it was found that the real rapist was already doing time for a series of other rapes.

Luther, even while inside, had been instrumental in helping Sheppard retain his sanity during his first year of incarceration. He had told Sheppard that being in prison didn't make a person guilty; it just meant the odds had been against him or her. And when that person knows of their innocence, they have nothing to be ashamed about. It had not come as a surprise to anyone that, after leaving prison, Luther had gone back to college and gotten his PhD in Social Work as well as become a minister.

It had become routine that when any of the young men Sheppard had mentored was released and had no family or friends to return to, Sheppard would recommend that they go to Luther. The agency Luther founded helped them ease back into society. It encouraged them to obtain college degrees, find meaningful employment and work hard to regain their dignity and self-respect. Over the years, she'd met with Luther on Sheppard's behalf a number of times. He'd even officiated their wedding. She agreed with Sheppard that Luther had a way of inspiring people.

She snuggled closer to him. "So, what's your plan?"

He chuckled. "Just like that? You're not going to try talking me out of anything?"

She leaned up on her elbow, then looked down at him and smiled. "Of course not. It's your life. I'm just along for the ride."

Sheppard hooked a hand around her to lower her head to his mouth. Her lips parted on contact and he slid his tongue inside. Carson had a way of making him feel as if he was the luckiest man on earth. Their tongues tangled relentlessly with a degree of passion that made his erection throb. Made every nerve-ending inside his body feel rejuvenated. When she moaned, he deepened the kiss, getting even more aroused by her taste.

He pulled back and stared into her beautiful mocha-colored face, gazing into her copper brown eyes beneath long curly lashes. "Don't you think we're getting too old for this?" he asked as his hand began moving up her inner thigh.

She chuckled. "Speak for yourself, Sheppard. Nobody told you to marry a younger woman."

He began stroking her between her legs, running his fingers through the curly hair covering her feminine mound, deliberately igniting a fire inside of her. "The difference in our ages bothered me at first."

He heard her sharp intake of breath when he eased a finger inside of her. "I know, but I refuse to allow you to let it. It was meant for us to be together," she said on a breathless whisper.

Sheppard truly believed that now, although he hadn't at the time. All he had to do was remember their beginning. One, he'd thought, could never have a happy ending. More than once he'd tried to convince her that she deserved someone else but she had refused to listen.

"Just remember that we're making up for lost time," she said breathlessly, as he worked his finger inside of her. His erection thickened. He felt hard and achy and loved making her come this way.

"We're doing anything and everything that we couldn't do then," she added, barely getting the words out.

A smile touched his lips. That was true. Was that the reason he was driven to make love to her every single day? Sometimes two or three times in the same day? Trying out positions he'd only dreamed about over the past fifteen years? Positions he had no business knowing about, let alone trying. "No more talking, sweetheart."

"You won't hear a complaint from me."

He eased her on her back and hovered over her, with his finger still firmly planted inside of her, while his thumb stroked her clitoris. He liked looking at the emotions on her face whenever he gave her pleasure. "You're ready for me to stop?"

"No."

He didn't think so. Arousing her could arouse him and he could feel his erection expand even more. She gazed into his eyes and the intensity did something to him. And then her body began quivering all over, especially the area between her legs. But he didn't stop and when she threw her head back and screamed his name, he lowered his mouth to hers, kissing her right into an orgasm.

#

An hour or so later, Sheppard was still awake, holding a deeply satisfied Carson in his arms. He was pretty damn satisfied himself. Multiple orgasms were something he'd never experienced before her. And at his age, who would have thought such a thing possible without some type of sex enhancing drug. The only drug he needed was lying here in his arms. His wife was pretty damn potent.

And as he lay there, inhaling the scent of their lovemaking and loving the feel of her naked body entwined with his, he couldn't help but reflect back, taking a stroll down memory lane to the time they'd met. The very first time he'd laid his eyes on Carson Boyett was a day that had changed his life forever.

PART ONE
THE PAST

The past can only be accepted.
It can't be forgotten, edited or erased.
And it can never be changed.
Anonymous

1

Sheppard, Warden Smallwood wants to see you."

Sheppard Granger nodded. "Okay, Ambrose. How's your mother?" he asked the prison guard.

Ambrose had told him last week that his elderly mother had slipped and fallen, breaking her hip. The guard had been very worried.

"They got her in rehab. She'll be there for another couple of weeks and then Kathie and I decided to move her in with us for a while."

"That might be a good idea," Sheppard said, walking alongside the man. "And how are Kathie and the boys?"

He knew Ambrose Cheney was thirty-six and had three young sons below the age of eleven. His wife Kathie was a school teacher. From the moment Sheppard had met Ambrose, he'd liked the younger man. Unlike some prison guards who let power go to their heads, Ambrose treated all the inmates with respect. In turn, Ambrose was well-liked and respected.

Sheppard wished he could say the same of some of the other guards, particularly Wayne Cullers. Everyone stayed out of Culler's way, including Sheppard. The only good thing about Cullers was that he'd be retiring in a few months. At least, that was the word among the prisoners. Sheppard hoped so.

"Everyone is fine," Ambrose said, breaking into his thoughts. "The boys are growing up fast. Eating me out of house and home. Kathie and I hope we'll be able to afford college when the time comes. Right now, the grocery bills are killing us."

Sheppard knew first-hand how much growing boys could eat. He thought about his own three sons. As always, thinking about them and what he'd missed out on over the last ten years caused a deep pain to settle around his heart. This was not how he thought his life would turn out. He should be sitting behind a huge desk at Granger Aeronautics and working with his staff as they went over the designs and developments of yet another aircraft. It had been hard adjusting to prison life, especially knowing he hadn't committed the crime he was doing time for.

"You're walking like you're in a hurry, Sheppard."

"Sorry about that." Ambrose was tall but not as tall as Sheppard and he slowed his stride so the younger man could keep up.

Sheppard had gotten transferred to Delvers from Glenworth a few months ago and was still trying to find his way around. When he had entered prison ten years ago, he'd been assigned to Glenworth Penitentiary, a place known to house mostly hardcore criminals. He had definitely been out of his element there and the first two years had been difficult. He'd come from a family of wealth and prestige. So, he'd been ill-equipped when he'd come up against men who'd grown up with nothing and resented him. He'd gotten roughed up a few times, threatened and bullied. But he had refused to be broken. It was only a miracle that during his third year, he'd shared a prison cell with a man name Luther Thomas.

Luther, who'd been wrong convicted of rape, had been instrumental in helping Sheppard retain his sanity. He was the one who'd encouraged him to use his skills as a business executive to help others and the two of them had come up with a plan. Together, he and Luther had begun programs in prison such as Toastmasters, Leaders of Tomorrow and the GED program. Their efforts had been successful and recognized by the media and even the governor.

They'd even implemented mentoring programs to turn around the lives of several inmates. Sheppard's strong points as a businessman had always been in strategic planning. With the warden's help, he'd put that well-honed skill to work by reaching out to several corporations and convincing them of the need for education and vocational training for inmates. As a result, several business classes had been instituted. By the time he'd left Glenworth, an inmate could get his associate degree in a number of fields, and Sheppard was glad that quite a number of young men had done so. For the past four years, he had received national attention when he'd been the recipient of the Born Leader award from the Governor's Commission on Prison Reform.

Several prisons around the country had wanted him to relocate to establish such programs at their facilities; however the decision had always been his to remain at a facility in Virginia, not far from home. With the governor's help, he'd established a number of satellite classes that connected inmates with well-known universities.

Sheppard was proud of all the men whose lives he had helped turn around. Those who were now free men were having positive impacts on their communities. Some had gone back to school, many even to college, and others were business owners—successful men.

Six months ago, upon the recommendation of the warden, the governor had approved Sheppard's transfer to Delvers, a prison located thirty-minutes from Glenworth, that housed less-serious offenders, mainly young men between the ages of eighteen and twenty-four. Sheppard was to work closely with Warden Smallwood as a trustee, initiating various projects to ensure that the less serious offenders didn't become serious ones in the future. He'd been assigned a team of twenty inmates to mentor, and working with the young men had made the days bearable. It was also good that Delvers had a warden who cared.

Sheppard liked Adam Smallwood. The man was a visionary with a huge heart. He was determined to decrease the length of time the inmates spent at his facility instead of trying to increase it. But more than anything, Smallwood wanted them to be productive citizens when they left Delvers. Sheppard whole-heartedly agreed with that concept.

And so, here he was, on his way to probably meet yet another young inmate needing his help. The administrative area was on another floor and located on the other side of the huge building. Sheppard didn't mind the long walk and tried to get in as much exercise as he could each day. He tried not to think about the fact that his home in Sutton Hills had its own gym. No one lived in the house now and his three sons, now grown men, had scattered.

In the beginning, it had been hard to be separated from his sons. They'd lost their mother and then months later, they'd lost him as well. He knew from his father how a number of their friends had turned their backs on the Granger boys because their parents wouldn't allow their kids to associate with the sons of a killer. Hearing that had been hard on Sheppard, and he could just imagine what all they'd gone through. Sadly, he used to call some of those same people friends. That was one of the reasons his sons had decided that they wouldn't return home after leaving Charlottesville for college.

Jace, his oldest son, who had been sixteen when Sheppard had left for prison, had finished law school and had taken a job in Los Angeles; Caden, who'd been fourteen, had also finished college and was pursuing his dream of being a musician. Last time they talked, Caden had told him that he'd joined a band--the Depots--as their saxophone player.

And then there was Dalton, his youngest son, who'd also gotten a college degree...just barely...and only because he had to maintain his grades to play football. That paid off when he'd been drafted to play professionally in the NFL after college. Dalton had been a few days shy of turning twelve when Sheppard had left. The youngest, he had often been referred to as Sylvia's baby and she had pretty much spoiled the boy rotten. Things had come too easily for Dalton and it was evident he was beginning to feel entitled. Sheppard knew from talking with his father that Dalton still had that mentality. Unlike Jace and Caden, who returned to Charlottesville occasionally to visit their grandfather, and who, over the years, came to visit Sheppard pretty regularly, his youngest son seldom came home.

According to his father, Dalton had pretty well walked away from his family. Then again, Sheppard was well aware that Richard had pretty much given up on Dalton, too, claiming he was as selfish as Sylvia had been and was living a wild life off the money he'd earned from his life as a professional football player. He was living in the fast lane and throwing away most of what he made on fast cars and faster women.

Richard Granger was convinced if his youngest grandson got his hands on his trust fund at twenty-five, he would squander it all. That was why Richard changed the terms of his will. Unlike Jace and Caden, who got access to their funds at twenty-five, Richard had amended Dalton's trust fund so that he couldn't get a penny out of it before he turned thirty. That action had pissed Dalton off to no end and he hadn't spoken to his grandfather since.

Jace was the only one who'd married, but according to Richard, even that was on shaky ground. As the oldest grandson, there had always been a special bond between Jace and Richard, and it hadn't surprised Sheppard that Jace had confided to Richard about the deplorable state of his marriage even though he never mentioned anything about it whenever he visited with Sheppard.

Sheppard figured it was mainly because Jace wouldn't want him to worry about anything. But Sheppard had news for him. When it came to his sons, he worried. He wished Jace and his wife Eve could work things out, but according to his father--who didn't like Eve anyway and hadn't wanted Jace to marry the woman--it would be for the best if they divorced. Richard claimed he'd never seen Jace so unhappy.

Sheppard had met Eve a few times when she'd accompanied Jace to see him. He'd tried to keep an open mind where the young woman was concerned. She had also come from a well-to-do family and had seemed pretty taken with Jace. But Sheppard knew his father was privy to information Jace hadn't shared with him.

Richard was already preparing for the worst and had taken steps to make sure that if and when Jace's marriage ended, Eve wouldn't leave with any more than she'd brought with her. Specifically, Richard Granger was making sure Eve didn't get her hands on any portion of Jace's trust fund.

Sheppard regretted the time he'd lost with his sons. It was time that could never be recaptured. Although he'd left them in his father's care and knew Richard had done the best he could with three teenagers, Sheppard had felt useless, knowing he couldn't do anything to help Jace, Caden or Dalton had they needed him.

However, the more he worked with the young men he mentored, the more he began to believe there was a reason he was here instead of sitting behind that huge desk at Granger Aeronautics. He wanted to believe that the man upstairs knew that he was needed for other young men who'd lost their way. Young men whose lives he could touch in a positive way. And he was probably about to find out about another one in a few minutes.

"You can go right on in," Ambrose said, cutting into his reverie when they reached Warden Smallwood office. "They are expecting you."

"They?" he asked. That was different. He looked at Ambrose in question. The man had worked at Delvers for twelve years, had started when it was a spanking new facility and Sheppard doubted very little happened that the man didn't know about.

"Yes. I figure he wants to introduce you Carson Boyett. Boyett's the attorney who's working closely with a few of the inmates to reopen their cases for recommendations for new trials and for consideration with the parole board for early releases."

"Oh, I see." He nodded. It made sense, then, for the warden to want him to meet the man. Chances were they would be working close together. He knew a number of the young men here had sentences that in his book were too severe for what they'd done.

Although Ambrose told him to just go on in, the professional in Sheppard, who'd once been the CEO of a multi-million dollar company, knocked anyway to let his presence be known.

"Come in Sheppard, we've been expecting you."

Sheppard walked in. His gaze first went to Warden Smallwood before switching to the woman sitting in the chair by his desk. She stood for a minute, and his mind went blank, almost totally missing what Smallwood was saying. But he came to his senses in time to hear the warden say, "Sheppard, I want you to meet Attorney Carson Boyett."

Carson Boyett was a woman. And a beautiful woman, at that. He knew it wasn't because his eyes were playing tricks on him, or the fact that being locked up behind bars didn't afford him the opportunity to mingle with women, except, of course, for those working within the walls of the prison. But as his sons would probably say, this woman was *hot*. And more than likely pretty damn young, which meant he had no business checking her out the way he was doing. But there was something going on between them that he hadn't counted on. Something he hadn't felt in ten years. Sexual chemistry and intense attraction. He could feel the vibes between them. And the attraction seemed to be mutual.

Carson Boyett was professionally dressed in a two-piece navy business suit and matching pumps. Her dark-brown hair was pinned up on her head in a neat and tidy looking knot. She possessed soft-looking mocha colored skin, a sensual pair of copper brown eyes, a cute pixie nose and a pair of full lips that curved in a smile.

She had to look up at him, so he figured her height was somewhere around five-feet-ten, compared to his six-three stature. Her body was curvaceous, which was evident in the pencil skirt she was wearing and her full breasts were outlined beneath her blouse and jacket.

Sheppard offered his hand while holding her gaze intently. "Nice meeting you, Attorney Boyett."

#

Carson had felt the full impact of Sheppard Granger's presence the moment he'd entered the room. A surge of total awareness had trickled through her body. She put his age at somewhere in his mid-forties. He was tall, probably a good six-foot-two or three inches, with dark brown eyes and black hair cut low on his head. She thought he had a masculine physique that could rival that of a much younger man, hands down.

CAPTIVATED BY LOVE

The man had stimulated her senses before uttering a single word. She'd heard about him. Both Warden Grady at Glenworth and Warden Smallwood had sung his praises for being a superb role model and leader.

That was all well and good, but why was he having such an impact on her? Why did the husky timbre of his voice seem to thicken the air between them? She was so aware of him as a man. His nearness. His scent. The heat of the hand holding hers. There was no way she could ignore the male power and strength radiating off him, but not in a threatening sort of way.

Standing up close before him, she noticed that his coloring was so smooth, it reminded her of the hot cocoa she'd had that morning. His high cheekbones, full lips, hawkish nose and chiseled jaw presented a stunningly handsome package. There was a brush of salt and pepper hair at his temples giving him an overall sexy and debonair look. He was wearing the typical inmate orange, but it didn't detract from his looks in any way.

She heard he'd been a CEO of a multi-million dollar company and it was obvious he was used to leading, not being led. Being in charge, being in control. Regardless of his clothes, this was a man who would stand out, and draw attention in a positive way. He was doing just that with his work with inmates. Even the governor hailed him as a strategic genius, which was why he was here at Delvers, implementing model programs to help inmates achieve their full potential. He was a man who could easily adapt to any given situation, and make the best of what he was dealt, while reaching out to others and making the best for them as well.

There was something about those dark eyes staring at her, causing her to feel a flutter in the pit of her stomach. And if that wasn't bad enough, she couldn't ignore the heat radiating between them. After her disastrous marriage to Pence Denmark, the last thing she'd allowed herself to be was affected by a man. But she was definitely attracted to Sheppard Granger. Although she hadn't lowered her guard, he'd managed to slip through a crack she hadn't realized was there.

And why did her hand feel so good in his? Besides the heat exuding from him, she felt something else. Something she preferred not putting a name to at the moment. "It's nice meeting you as well, Mr. Granger," she said, finally finding her voice. "I've heard a lot of wonderful things about you, from a number of people, including both Warden Grady and Warden Smallwood. And *especially* Craig Long. He's forever singing your praises." Craig Long was an eighteen-year-old that Sheppard mentored. More than likely, he was aware that Craig's parents had hired her to push for a new trial.

Sheppard Granger finally released her hand and the smile that touched his lips had her stomach churning. "Craig's a good kid. He doesn't belong in here."

She nodded. "I agree and I'm working hard to get his conviction overturned. It's obvious he confessed under duress."

At that moment, Warden Smallwood cleared his throat as if to remind them of his presence. "Sheppard, Attorney Boyett is working on the Long case as well as that of several others you're mentoring. I'd like for you to meet with her over the next few weeks to go over the list I gave you."

"Sure thing, Warden Smallwood," Sheppard said smiling.

"And I would also love to have her sit in with us when we draw up our plans," the warden said, nodding in her direction. "In addition to representing several of the young men in here, she also volunteers her time teaching some of our classes. Chances are, you'll be seeing a lot of her around here."

Sheppard glanced back at her and immediately she felt desire claw at her under the scrutiny of his intense dark brown eyes. "I'm looking forward to meeting with you, Attorney Boyett."

A smile touched her lips. "Likewise, Mr. Granger."

2

C arson walked into her friend Roddran Malloy's hospital room. Roddran smiled the moment she saw her and asked excitedly, "Did you see her!"

Carson couldn't help but return her best friend's smile. "Yes, Rod, she's beautiful; a combination of both you and Myles."

Roddran's blue eyes sparked and her smile widened even more. "Please tell that to Myles when you see him. He's already claiming total ownership in the looks department. He says she looks nothing like me."

"I will make it my business to do that."

Carson had met Roddran when she first moved to Charlottesville years ago. They had arrived in town about the same time, both due to job offers. Carson had gone to work for the State Attorney's office, while Roddran had accepted a job with the Public Defender's office. More than once, they'd faced off in the court room, yet had somehow become good friends. Roddran's husband, Myles, was also an attorney and worked for a law firm in town. Carson had been at Roddran's wedding after Myles had finally convinced her that marrying him was the best thing that could ever happen to her. Carson had agreed and told Roddran so. That had been close to five years ago.

"I can't wait to leave here and take my baby home," Roddran said, interrupting Carson's thoughts.

"Hey, you had a C-section, so take it easy. You'll leave soon enough. Don't rush things."

"I know. I know. I'm just so dang happy."

Carson could tell and she refused to let the regrets she'd had dampen her happiness for her friend. But still, she couldn't push to the back of her mind the thought that had her baby lived, he or she would be celebrating their fourteenth birthday.

"Carson?"

She glanced over at Roddran. "Yes?"

"You're thinking about your own baby, aren't you?"

There was no way she could lie to Roddran. "Yes. Had my baby lived, he or she would be a teenager. Imagine that."

"You married young. At twenty."

Yes, she had married young, mainly because she hadn't wanted to be alone after her aunt died. She had lost both her parents at fifteen when a man had robbed the bookstore they owned and decided not to leave any witnesses behind. She had been at school at the time and would never forget the day she'd been called to the principal's office and told the news of her parents' death by her mom's sister, her aunt Michelle. Her aunt had become

35

her guardian and then died of breast cancer less than five years later. She had met Pence a week after her aunt's funeral at a coffee shop.

"Yes, I married young and was pregnant at twenty-three. I thought my life was perfect but Pence showed me just how wrong I was."

"But at least you made changes afterward."

"Yes, I did." After her divorce from Pence, she had been determined to make it on her own. And with the help of the scholarships she'd received, she had gone to college and law school, graduating at the top of her law class.

"Let's not talk about my ex," she said, smiling over at Roddran.

"Okay, how are things going at work?"

"Great. I think I will be able to get Craig Long's conviction overturned. Judge Witherspoon is reviewing the case now." Then Carson proceeded to update her friend on all the other cases she was working on. She had left the State Attorney's office four years ago and opened her own law practice. Things had been hard in the beginning. She'd lived in the red that first year but now she was seeing a healthy profit. That allowed her to do the pro bono work at the prison that she enjoyed so much.

Her thoughts turned to Sheppard Granger. The man definitely had a lasting effect on her. Since meeting him last week, he'd been on her mind. Too much. There was no doubt that she'd been deeply attracted to him. How crazy was that? She was attracted to a convict.

"You okay? You're sitting over there with a funny look on her face."

She glanced over at Roddran. "Yes, I'm fine. I was just thinking about a guy I met last week."

"A handsome guy?"

"Yes, definitely."

"Well, did he ask you out?"

Carson chuckled. No need to tell Roddran there was no way he could do that because he was in jail. "No, it was a business meeting. But I could tell he was interested, too." Not that it mattered, since nothing could ever come of the attraction. She hoped it settled down before they saw each other again. They were scheduled to meet again in a couple of weeks. She felt a stirring in her stomach just thinking about it.

"Will you see him again?"

She glanced over at Roddran. "Yes, we have another business meeting set up."

"Good. "I'm counting on you to make your move on him then."

She started to tell Roddran that it wouldn't be that kind of meeting, but decided not to. At least, not today. One day, she would tell her best friend about her fantasies and the man starring in them. She would also tell Roddran why they were just that. Fantasies.

"When have you known me to make a move on any man, Roddran?"

A huge smile touched her best friend's lips. "But there is a first time for everything. I'm not giving up on you Carson."

Yes, there was a first time for everything. But Carson doubted she would ever make such a move, especially on Sheppard Granger.

#

"Ready for your meeting with Attorney Boyett?"

Sheppard glanced up from his book. Reading was his favorite pastime and whenever he could, he would go to the library and use the computer, determined to keep up with what was going on in the world. He might not be out there in it, but that didn't mean he didn't want to be kept informed. His father had arranged for Sheppard's favorite news and business magazines to be delivered to him at the prison and he appreciated that.

He was very much aware the country was in a war, and knew who were the Super Bowl and NBA Champs.. He kept up with all the political news, arts and entertainment, business and technology. He'd always been an avid reader and refused to let that go now.

Sheppard had doubled the number of articles he'd read over the past three weeks, mainly to keep one particular person from intruding into his thoughts. The very person he was to meet with today. "Yes, I'm ready." The moment he said the words, he knew they were not true. He doubted he was ready to see Attorney Carson Boyett again...even after three weeks.

Sheppard began walking beside Ambrose to the media room where the meeting would take place. He hated leaving the library, which was one of the few areas with windows. The bars were a constant reminder of where he was.

He'd gotten emails today from some of the guys he'd mentored while at Glenworth. Most had served their time and had gotten released right before he'd left. He always enjoyed hearing from Lamar "Striker" Jennings, Quasar Patterson and Stonewall Courson, not to mention the others: Andrew Logan, Ryker Valentine, Locke Dangerfield, Shogun Duke and Macayle Wasilla. They were men who'd served their time and were now making something of their lives.

"How are things going with that Fontane kid?" Ambrose asked him.

Sheppard drew in a deep, troubling breath. He'd been at Delvers for only two weeks when Matthew Fontane had arrived, furious, full of anger and mad at the world. At eighteen, Fontane had been caught in a carjacking ring. The driver had suddenly had a heart attack and would have died if Fontane hadn't stayed behind to give the man CPR. For that, he'd received a lighter sentence than the others. However, Fontane felt he should have been able to walk free. The warden had assigned him to Shep's team, and they had butted heads from day one. They were still butting heads.

"Rather slowly, Ambrose. But I've dealt with worse," he said, thinking mainly about some of the other kids he'd mentored while at Glenworth. Fontane only had five years. That was nothing, compared to some of the guys he'd seen at Glenworth. Some of them were looking at a forty-year or more stretch. Sheppard had twenty more to go himself.

"But you won't give up on him?"

Sheppard glanced over at Ambrose. "I can't. Deep down, Fontane's a good kid. Otherwise he wouldn't have risked getting arrested just to stay back and keep that man alive. Once I get him to realize that, regardless of his good deed, a crime was committed, he'll be alright."

"I hope so. He's been nothing but trouble since he arrived here."

Sheppard knew all about the trouble Fontane was causing. The young man seemed to thrive on getting into fights and spewing profanity at the prison guards. Getting through to Fontane wouldn't be easy, but he was determined to turn the kid around.

The moment he and Ambrose rounded the corner to where the media room was located, Sheppard could smell Attorney Boyett. It was the same perfume she'd been wearing that day. A scent that could boggle a man's mind, although it didn't seem to bother Ambrose. "Can you smell perfume?"

Ambrose lifted a brow. "No. What I smell is all that tar they're using to repair the roof."

Sheppard said nothing as they continued walking. The scent of tar was not what was getting absorbed into his nostrils. Evidently, Attorney Boyett's scent was meant just for him. He shook his head, wondering why he would think such a thing.

If he were truthful with himself, he would have to admit he'd been thinking of a lot of weird things when it came to Carson Boyett. He went to sleep thinking about her each night, remembering her smile, the way she would look at him when she wasn't aware that he knew she was doing so.

Their first meeting hadn't lasted more than an hour. Yet, it had been long enough for him to conclude that any man would appreciate having her as a lifelong partner. He had checked out her hand and hadn't seen a ring, but that didn't mean she wasn't seriously involved with anyone.

And why did such a thing matter to him? It wasn't like he was available. Even though he was not guilty of the crime he'd been accused of, he was still behind bars. A man without freedom. The only positive thing right now was that his father had hired this top-notch investigator by the name of Marshall Imerson to see about clearing his name. The last time Imerson had visited him, he seemed excited about some things he'd uncovered and was digging deeper. Just the thought that his wife's real killer could be exposed gave Shep hope. He still held on to the possibility that one day, his sentence would get overturned and he would walk out of there a free man.

He paused when they reached the door, moving aside to let Ambrose open it. Attorney Boyett stood when they entered the windowless room. "Ambrose. Mr. Granger," she acknowledged.

Ambrose smiled. "Attorney Boyett. I'll be over here if you need me." He then crossed the room and sat down in a chair.

"Attorney Boyett. How are you today?" Sheppard said, entering the room.

She smiled. "Fine and you, Mr. Granger?"

"I'm doing okay. Thanks for asking."

She nodded. "I thought today we should meet on Matthew Fontane."

He lifted a brow. "What about Fontane?"

"There's a problem. Can we sit down to discuss it?"

"Sure."

She sat down and he tried not to notice how the hem of her skirt raised a little, giving him a glimpse of her thigh. Today she was wearing another business suit, this one olive green, with matching pumps. Unlike the other day, when her hair had been pinned up on her head, today it was hanging down past her shoulders. She had a lot of it and the thick dark-brown strands looked silky to the touch. He could imagine running his hands through them.

"Now then," she said, opening a folder on the desk. "I see that you meet with him twice a week and have done so for the past two months."

"Yes, that's right." He leaned back in his chair. If he sat too close to her, he would be tempted to reach out and touch her. He wondered just how young she was, though he guessed her to be in her early thirties.

"How that's been going?"

He rubbed his hand down his face, feeling a little frustrated. Why was he wasting his time being attracted to a woman he couldn't have? Being attracted to any woman period? "Fine. Why do you want to know about Fontane?"

She glanced up at him and their gazes met and held a minute. "The family of the man whose life he saved wants to do whatever they can to help reduce his sentence."

Sheppard nodded. "That's good news."

"I think so, too. The only problem is that Fontane can't seem to keep out of trouble. As a result, the parole board has refused their request."

Sheppard knew that wasn't news Fontane would want to hear. "Anyway they'll change their minds?"

"I doubt it. But what I can do is request another hearing in six month's time, to see if his behavior has improved. If it has, they might reconsider."

"I'm sure that would mean a lot to him, Attorney Boyett."

"We'll see. I just wanted you to know, so when you meet with him again, you can strongly suggest he starts improving his attitude."

"Okay, I will do that."

"Great. And while I have you here, I thought we could discuss Amari Carmen and Rourke Blackman. If things continue to improve with them, I might be able to get the last year of their sentences reduced to community service."

"That would be great!"

They spent the next hour or so going over her other cases. More than once, she'd caught him staring at her. Then at other times, he would glance over and catch her staring at him. When that happened, she'd quickly turn her attention back to the files in front of her. The last thing he wanted was to make her nervous. Although Ambrose was in the room, Sheppard had noticed the prison guard had taken a crossword puzzle out from his pocket. The guard seemed far more interested in doing his puzzle than witnessing Shep and Attorney Boyett's inability to keep their eyes off each other.

"Well, that's it, Mr. Granger. I appreciate your time."

"Time is what I seem to have a lot of these days," he said standing. "I'd like to ask you something though."

She stood as well. "What?"

"Why do you do this? I understand you have a nice law firm in Charlottesville, yet you spend a lot of time here. Why?"

She smiled. "My parents were community activists and I learned a lot from them. I lost them when I was fifteen. There was a robbery that went very wrong at the bookstore they owned."

"Sorry to hear that."

"Thank you. I recall that one of my dad's pet peeves was the number of petty crimes that could land a person in jail for life without any chance of parole. He felt the system sometimes created criminals instead of rehabilitating them. So, over the years, it became one of my causes. I decided to work within the system to make changes, anyway I could. I feel that's the least I can do to honor my father's memory."

Ten minutes later, Sheppard was walking with Ambrose, back toward the area where his cell was located. He was lost in thoughts about Carson when Ambrose said, "She's something else, isn't she?"

He heard the admiration in Ambrose's voice. "Who? Attorney Boyett?"

"Yes. She's been coming around for about four years. Before that, she worked out of Glenworth. All pro bono. I'm surprised your paths never crossed."

Maybe it was a good thing that they hadn't, Sheppard thought. "Glenworth is a big place."

"I know. I turned down a job offer there. I figured the warden and I wouldn't get along. That was before Warden Grady. I understand he's been doing great things the five years he's been there."

"He has." There was no need to tell Ambrose how he'd butted heads with the former warden at Glenworth, Warden Fisher, many times.

"Do you know if Attorney Boyett is married? I noticed she's not wearing a wedding ring."

"She's divorced. My wife knows someone who used to work with her at the State Attorney's Office. Attorney Boyett made a name for herself when she took on a high profile case. Even put her life on the line in doing so."

"What happened?"

"A cop discovered some of his fellow officers were on the take. Before he could blow the whistle, he was framed and sent to prison for fifteen years at Glenworth. His wife hired Attorney Boyett to get him a new trail. She did. The man had served three years before finally leaving prison a free man, but not before the bad cops murdered his wife and tried killing Attorney Boyett as well."

Sheppard felt a sharp pain around his heart. "I hope they got the bastards."

"They did. All the cops responsible were arrested and are now serving time."

Sheppard's heart went out to the man who'd lost his wife. Then, knowing that Attorney Boyett could have lost her life as well, his heart started pounding. At least those responsible were behind bars.

At that moment he couldn't help but think about the person who'd killed his wife, Sylvia. Her murderer was still out there.

He knew everyone assumed he was Sylvia's killer. The prosecution had convinced the jury that he'd been having an affair and killed his wife when she refused to give him a divorce. The truth was just the opposite. Sylvia was the one who'd been involved in a number of affairs. At first, he figured she'd been killed by one of her lovers, but the more he'd thought about it, the more he believed her death had nothing to do with her extramarital affairs but was instead a cover-up for something bigger. Exactly what, he wasn't sure. But that was the reason he and his father had hired a private investigator. There was more to this story than anyone knew. And he was counting on Marshall Imerson to uncover the truth.

#

Long after Ambrose and Sheppard Granger had left, Carson continued to sit in the windowless room alone, absorbed in her thoughts while trying to regain her composure. She was determined to figure out why a man like Sheppard Granger had such a profound effect on her.

She was a logical person. And in this situation, she needed to be rational. Carson had to figure out what there was about Sheppard Granger that made her lose all coherent thought, the common sense she was born with and the self-protective wall she'd erected around herself since her divorce.

Since meeting Sheppard Granger, she couldn't get him out of her thoughts, her dreams. That's why she'd been nervous about meeting with him today. She'd been determined to prove to herself that all those emotions regarding him were merely figments of her imagination. After their meeting today, she wasn't sure that was all it was. After all, the man was fascinating to the eyes, well-built and well-mannered. Then there was something else. She believed that he was a man who would hurt himself before hurting anyone else. That puzzled her, since he was locked up for the murder of his wife. However, for some reason, that charge just didn't seem to fit him.

If her assumptions were wrong about a man, it wouldn't be the first time. They'd definitely been wrong about Pence Denmark, and she had the scars to prove it. She'd only been a few weeks shy of her twentieth birthday when she'd met Pence. From their initial meeting, he'd come across as the perfect gentleman--suave, charming and so polite. Within six months, they'd married and she thought they would live happily ever after.

Within months, however, she'd found out just how wrong she was about him. The only good thing that had come from her marriage had been her in-laws. Stanley and Emma Denmark had been the best and wouldn't hesitate to call out their only child regarding his mistreatment of her. Pence often accused her of turning his parents against him.

She had wanted to retain her close relationship with them after the divorce, but he wouldn't allow it. To keep peace between Pence and his parents, she'd left Florida.

Although she missed the close relationship she'd shared with her in-laws, it had been a good decision. She'd heard that Pence had remarried a year after their divorce.

She stood and began pacing when her thoughts shifted back to Sheppard. During their meeting, the sexual tension between them had been obvious each and every time their gazes collided. She wouldn't have been surprised if Ambrose hadn't picked up on it. And at the end, when they'd shaken hands, something akin to a throbbing sensation had swept through her.

She drew in a sharp breath, knowing she had to put a stop to this mental madness about Sheppard Granger. There was no way she would allow anything to develop between them. Regardless of her intense attraction to him, she was too old for fantasies.

#

"You wanted to see me old man?"

Sheppard glanced up when Matthew Fontane entered the room. "Yes, have a seat, Matthew."

"And what if I said that I preferred standing?"

Sheppard drew in a deep breath, determined not to let Fontane rattle him. Others had tried and failed. All he had to do was think about Striker and Stonewall. If those two hadn't succeeded in rattling him, no one could. "Suit yourself."

"So why did you want to see me?" Fontane asked again.

"I might have some good news to share with you,"

Like he figured it would, that got Fontane's attention. "What?"

"You might be leaving here sooner than planned."

He watched the young man's eyes light up. "About damn time. When do I start packing?"

"Nothing is final. It depends on your attitude around here and--"

"Whoa, wait a fucking minute," Fontane cut in to say. "I don't plan to start jumping through hoops for anybody. I didn't do anything wrong. If it wasn't for me, that old bastard would be dead. I stayed back to help his ass. I shouldn't even be in here."

Sheppard just stared at Fontane. The two of them had been meeting periodically now for months and Fontane just couldn't accept the fact he was just as guilty as those who'd run off but were eventually caught. The only difference was that he'd shown he had something his friends lacked—a conscience. That was why his pals were doing fifteen years and he'd only gotten five. But for Fontane to continue to think that he shouldn't be serving *any* time, that was preposterous.

"You know what, Matthew? One day, you're going to accept that nobody owes you anything. Like the rest of us, you have to prove your worth, make good on your given situation and--"

"Don't hand me all that bullshit. You're a fine one to talk, Mr. Use-To-Be-CEO. You might not mind your freedom being taken away but I do. I hate it here. I hate the guards watching me all the time. I hate not being able to even piss in private. I hate the damn food I'm eating. I damn well hate all of you. So don't tell me about how I have to act just to get out of here. I will act any damn way I please." Then in an act of rebellion, Fontane kicked over the chair he'd refused to sit in.

Sheppard was up in a flash and grabbed Fontane by the collar, shoving him into the chair he'd vacated. "Is that what you think, Fontane, just because I refuse to act the ass like you do? That I like being here and having my freedom taken away? Well, let me tell you how wrong you are. I left behind three sons. Three sons who needed me. Three sons I miss like hell, each and every single day. But like a lot of the other guys in here, I'm trying to make the best of the situation. None of us likes this place any more than you do, but we're dealing with it, and I suggest you do the same and stop whining."

"I won't deal with it."

"Then you'll be responsible for whatever happens," Sheppard said, hating the way Fontane's nasty attitude was affecting other inmates.

"And it will be my business, old man. Not yours." Fontane jerked himself out of the chair and stalked to the door. When he opened it, a prison guard stood there waiting to escort him back to his cell.

"Not sure if that kid will ever come around," Ambrose said, reminding Sheppard of his presence in the room

Sheppard didn't say anything for a long minute. "He will eventually, Ambrose. Maybe not in time to get an early release, but hopefully before his five years are up. I refuse to give up on him."

Fontane wasn't the first young man to try and push his buttons and probably wouldn't be the last. But Shep would get through to him, eventually, the same way he'd gotten through to all the others. The rewards of hanging in there were worth it, especially when he saw how well the majority of them were doing. And what he liked more than anything was that the guys stayed in contact with him. They came to visit him from time to time to let him know how well they were doing. And those who couldn't visit would contact Sheppard through email to let him know where they were and that they were okay. Those men had become his surrogate family. They had helped him to endure his time behind bars just like he'd helped them.

"You're a man with a lot of patience, Sheppard. Not everyone would put in the time."

He told Ambrose what he'd told Attorney Boyett earlier that day. "Time is what I seem to have a lot of these days."

3

Biting her bottom lip while her fingers gripped tight on the handle of her briefcase, Carson ignored the loud clicking of her heels on the tile floor as she quickly walked through the halls of the prison's administration building. With every step, she tried to downplay the pounding of her heart, the escalation of her pulse and the erratic sound of her breathing.

She tried convincing herself that her anxious state had nothing to do with Sheppard Granger and the fact they would be meeting again today. It had been three weeks since their last meeting and he'd constantly been on her mind. It hadn't helped matters when she'd decided to go online and uncover every single thing she could about him...about the time before he was accused of murdering his wife. As far as she was concerned, anything after that was marred with sensationalism--media attempts at gaining high ratings. She wanted to know what the press had thought of Sheppard Granger when he'd still been the golden boy. After reading about all his accomplishments, she thought of him more as the Boy Wonder.

Born Sheppard Maceo Granger forty-seven years ago; closer to forty-eight since he had a birthday coming up in a month or so, he was the son of Richard and Ava Granger and was heir to the Granger empire. He'd had a baby brother who'd died at birth when Sheppard had been four. That baby had been named Jace; the name Sheppard had passed on to his firstborn son.

Sheppard had graduated from high school at sixteen, got his MBA at twenty, married at twenty-one and became a parent at twenty-two. His wife, the former Sylvia Gadling, had come from a wealthy Boston family. From the pictures she'd seen of them together, Sylvia's stunning beauty and his jaw-dropping handsomeness had made them a striking couple.

He'd received possibly every business award imaginable, on both a local and national level. And each time, his wife had been by his side to glow in his success. What was even more impressive was that he'd become known for always doing his best to give back to his community. His company was always in the forefront to support any and all worthwhile causes.

The articles showed photographs of Sheppard in his early twenties and through his late thirties. She didn't know of any man whose looks got better with age.

When Carson reached the door to the media room, she paused and drew in a deep, calming breath. She had assured herself before she'd left her office that she would be more in control when she saw him, but had a feeling that was wishful thinking. She should have called and cancelled today's meeting. She'd started to do that a number of times, already. What was the point in meeting him today when all she would do is sit there and practically drool while her panties got wet? She shook her head. No matter what, she would not let her attraction to Sheppard Granger be her downfall.

Opening the door, she swallowed the moment she saw him sitting at the table. Looking across the room, she saw Ambrose sitting in a chair in the corner. Both men stood upon seeing her.

"Sorry I'm late. Traffic from town was a little crazy today," she apologized.

"No harm done, Attorney Boyett," Ambrose said.

She noted Sheppard Granger hadn't said anything, but was just standing there, staring at her. Nervously pasting a smile on her face, she figured the best thing to do would be to get right down to business. "Mr. Granger, I thought we could cover--"

"Sheppard. Since we'll be doing a number of these meetings, it's okay for you to call me Sheppard."

She nodded while placing her briefcase on the table. "Okay. Please call me Carson."

A smile spread across his lips. The same lips she'd dreamed of kissing just last night. The same smile that could make heat curl in her stomach. "Okay, Carson."

And why did he have to say her name like that? In a way that heightened her already irregular pulse? "Then let's get started."

He looked at the files she was pulling out of her briefcase. "So what do you have for me today?" he asked.

Not what I wish I could have for you. She was tempted to spank her cheeks for thinking such a thing. At that moment, she knew today's meeting was going to be more difficult than ever.

#

Sheppard tried keeping his lustful thoughts at bay, but every time his gaze connected with Carson's, even for the briefest moment, jolts of sexual energy pounded his midsection. He was keenly aware of her in every pore of his body. Being this close to her was causing desire to race up his spine, and her scent seemed to thicken the very air he was breathing.

Although they were sitting a decent amount of space from each other at the table, more than once their legs accidently touched. The first time, he'd quickly apologized, since he'd been stretching out his leg when it happened. The contact made his body throb and when he caught her eyes, he couldn't ignore the look he saw--pure sexual awareness.

The next time, she had been the one to accidently touch her leg against his. Unexpectedly, he'd drawn in a sharp breath and barely heard her quick, "Sorry." He'd been tempted to tell her not to apologize, that she could brush her leg against his any time.

Avoiding the temptation of playing footsy with her, he straightened in his seat and decided to keep his legs to himself. The last thing he wanted to be accused of was any kind of sexual harassment.

"So, did you get a chance to talk to Matthew Fontane?" she asked him, breaking into his thoughts.

He glanced at her and a crackle of energy passed between them. He was surprised Ambrose hadn't heard the pop. But when he glanced over at where the guard sat, Ambrose appeared absorbed in his crossword puzzle, as usual.

He drew in a deep breath. "Yes, but I'm not sure he understands how important it will be for him to stay out of trouble."

"Well, let's hope it sinks in. The parole board meets in a couple of months."

"I'll be meeting with Fontane again this week and will reiterate it to him."

"Great."

It was evident they were stalling instead of bringing the meeting to an end. It was supposed to only last an hour and already, they'd gone thirty minutes beyond that time.

"When will we meet again?" he asked. What he was really asking though, was when he would see her again.

She shrugged her delicate shoulders. Today she was wearing another business suit. Another style, another color but just as professional and sexy. He liked this red one. She didn't know it but red was his favorite color. On her, it looked just like it was supposed to look. Red hot.

"When do you think we need to meet again, Sheppard?"

"In two weeks." He was suggesting two weeks instead of three because he honestly didn't think he could stand waiting three weeks.

She held his gaze and the spike of heat flowing between them caught him low in the gut. They continued to stare at each other for a few moments longer and then she nodded. "Okay. There's an important case I'm working on but I should be able to meet again with you in two weeks. I'll make the necessary arrangements with Warden Smallwood." She began gathering the files to put back in her briefcase.

Ambrose looked up from his puzzle. "The two of you are finished?"

Not by a long shot, Sheppard was tempted to say. "Yes, we're through for today."

#

Just like she'd done at the end of the last meeting, Carson deliberately stayed behind, saying she had a couple of files she needed to review.

CAPTIVATED BY LOVE

It was only after they left, closing the door behind them that she released a deep breath, convinced the manly scent of Sheppard still lingered in the air. During the meeting, she had to fight not to lose herself in the flicker of arousal she saw in the depths of his dark eyes. And when he had brushed his legs against hers, she had felt every cell in her body actually vibrate.

She stood and began pacing. Typically, her meetings never ran long but today's had gone half an hour later. In reality, she knew it probably could have ended sooner, but more than once there had been a lag in their conversation when they'd been caught staring at each other. And she'd found herself repeating information more than once about something when her concentration wavered.

The sound of his voice mesmerized her. Smooth yet husky, with the ability to caress her skin with each and every syllable. And whenever he smiled at her, she would feel all bubbly inside and would automatically smile back. Both of their mouths had to be aching from smiling at each other so much.

And why on earth had she agreed to see him again in two weeks instead of three? Deep down, Carson knew the answer. He wanted to see her again as much as she wanted to see him. Why would a level-headed thirty-seven-year-old woman want to become involved with a man ten years her senior, who was in prison with twenty more years to serve, a minimum of eight more before he could even be considered for parole? A man, who could very well be a murderer.

She stopped pacing and shook her head. She refused to believe that. She might not have known Sheppard Granger long but she doubted he was capable of killing anyone.

Carson began pacing again. Could the reason that she was so attracted to Sheppard have anything to do with the fact she hadn't seriously been involved with anyone for years?

It had taken her six years after her divorce to even consider getting serious about a guy. She had dated a race car driver name Gil Joyner for six months. She broke things off with him when his controlling tendencies became too much for her. After that, she only dated when she wanted to and usually her interest was in professional men--other attorneys, college professors, accountants and bankers. Men who didn't have a problem treating her as an equal.

Carson had taken enough crap from Pence not to ever want to be bothered with dominating males. She'd been happy and satisfied with the way her life was going...until the day she'd been introduced to Sheppard.

Something had to give. No, something had to stop. The whole idea of her being attracted so deeply to a convict didn't make any sense. Regardless of how good he looked, how wonderful he smelled, or how well he carried himself.

She needed to go home, soak in a bubble bath and have a glass of wine. She didn't care if it was the middle of the day. There were some things you just couldn't put off doing. And the one thing she wouldn't do, no matter how tempting, was to see Sheppard more often. Doing so served no purpose and might put ideas in his head she rather not have there.

She would see him again in three weeks, as she'd originally agreed. Hopefully, by then, she'd find a way to deal with the intense attraction she felt for Sheppard Granger.

#

Sheppard glanced at the illuminated clock on his wall. It was midnight and the guards had given the signal that all inmates were in their cells and accounted for. Most of them shared cells but one of the perks of being a trustee was having your own space. He had solid walls on both sides that afforded him some semblance of privacy. Still, the bedroom he'd left behind at Sutton Hills was a hundred times the size of the living/sleeping quarters he occupied now.

Now that all the guys on his floor were asleep, he should be able to close his eyes for the night as well. It was as if they were his responsibility, his surrogate sons, and until he knew they were safe for the night, he couldn't rest.

It had been that way when he'd been at Glenworth as well. A lot of the men had been bad asses but by the time they'd been released, they had managed to look at the world and their situation through new eyes. They hadn't been bitter, but better. Resilient, instead of resentful. Filled with humility instead of being consumed by hate. And he was proud of each and every one of them. Parting ways had been hard. At Delvers, he hoped he could make a difference in the lives of the twenty young men on his team. He cared about them.

His thoughts switched to Carson Boyett. He knew she cared about them as well. Otherwise, she wouldn't be putting in all those pro bono hours here. According to Ambrose--who'd had a wealth of information about Carson to share again--she had a small law practice in downtown Charlottesville.

Today, he'd been even more attracted to her than the last time. The scent of her perfume had been too damn nice, and his hand had itched to smooth back the one stray strand of hair that curled on her forehead. She'd worn her hair down today, touching her shoulders and he liked that style on her. It was hard to believe she was thirty-seven. She looked a whole lot younger than that. He would have guessed she was in her late twenties or so.

More than once, he'd been tempted to reach out and deliberately touch her hand when she'd handed him several documents. He appreciated that Ambrose followed the rules and never left them alone. No telling what moves he'd be tempted to make if he ever got her to himself.

Drawing in a deep breath, he shifted his head on the pillow. He knew that was wishful thinking. He wouldn't make any inappropriate moves on her, or any woman. He was raised to be too much of a gentleman for that. But still, Carson had a way of tempting him to the nth degree. The only moves he would ever make on her were in his dreams and knew the moment he closed his eyes, she'd be there, starring in each and every dream.

He had settled in a deep sleep when suddenly the bright lights woke him the same time the siren sounded. Had someone tried to escape? He quickly went to the front of the cell to see what was going on. Guards were running all over the place and he was able to ask one what was happening.

"One of the inmates pretended to have stomach pains. When the guard went into his cell to check on him, the inmate knocked him out and escaped. Luckily he was apprehended before he made it to the third floor."

Unease seeped inside Sheppard's every pore. "How's the guard?"

"He'll have a doozy of a headache in the morning, but other than that, he's okay."

"Can you tell me the name of the inmate who did it?" Sheppard asked, already having an idea who the person was but needing verification.

"Yeah. It was that troublemaker. Matthew Fontane."

4

Sheppard smiled as he read the email he'd received from Lamar "Striker" Jennings. Striker wanted him to know that he'd met all the requirements to get his Bachelor's Degree from Hampton University and intended to keep going and work on a MBA from the University of Virginia.

He couldn't be more proud of Striker. The young man had come a long way and Sheppard could see him going further. Same thing for Quasar Patterson and Stonewall Courson. After a rough beginning, those three had become the best of friends. When they'd left Glenworth, they'd promised to always have each other's backs. He believed they would.

The three had moved to Charlottesville, where Stonewall was born and where his sister and grandmother still lived. Sheppard figured he and Stonewall had bragged so much about what a great city Charlottesville was that Striker and Quasar wanted to check it out for themselves.

"Shep, there's someone here to see you."

Sheppard glanced over at Ambrose. "Thanks." He couldn't help wondering who would pay him a visit. He'd spoken to his father two days ago when Richard had called to let him know he had a business trip to Puerto Rico and wouldn't be back until next week. He doubted any of his sons would drop in for a surprise visit. Jace was in California, Caden was currently on the road with his band, and as far as Dalton was concerned, there was no telling. The good thing about Dalton playing in the NFL was that he could watch the games on television in the recreation room.

Sheppard had been proud of the way his son performed and knew he was doing okay with endorsements. Now if Dalton could only leave all those women alone and make sure he put some money aside for a rainy day, his youngest son would be fine.

As he continued to walk beside Ambrose to where inmates would meet with visitors, he wondered again who his visitor might be. His testosterones kicked into gear at the thought it might be Carson. But there was no way she'd pay him a random visit. He'd seen her a week ago and was counting the days until he would see her again. Deep down, he knew he shouldn't be all into her, when his future for the next twenty-years was inside these barricaded walls. But for some reason, he couldn't stop thinking about her.

"Wait here until I get him signed in," Ambrose said.

"Him?" he asked, trying to hide the disappointment in his voice.

Ambrose chuckled. "Yes. Him. Were you expecting a lady friend or something, Shep?"

Sheppard shrugged and returned the chuckle. "A man can hope, right?"

"Right. There's nothing wrong with hoping."

Sheppard sat down at the table in the media room, not the place where he'd met with Carson last week. In a way that was good. He didn't want to deal with any memories today.

He'd only been there ten minutes when the door opened. He stood when the private investigator his father had hired walked in behind Ambrose. "Marshall? This is a pleasant surprise."

Marshall Imerson had met with him a couple of times since Richard had hired him, mainly to gather information for his investigation.

"Sorry to bother you but I need to run some names by you. Can you tell me if any of them ring a bell?"

\#

Carson entered the restaurant and glanced around until she saw the man sitting at the table on the other side of the room. He sat there as if in deep thought and she could just imagine what was on his mind. Had his wife lived, they would be celebrating her thirtieth birthday tonight.

CAPTIVATED BY LOVE

Carson recalled the first time she'd met Roland. He'd been a cop intentionally set up by fellow corrupt cops to take the fall. As a result, he had been sentenced to fifteen years. He had served three years when his wife, Becca, had hired Carson to fight to have his case reopened. In retaliation, Becca was killed and an attempt had even been made on Carson's life. Carson had managed to expose the team of bad cops and in the end, all five had been charged with Becca's murder.

She would never forget the day when Becca Summers walked through the doors of the State Attorney's office where she'd worked. Becca had wanted help in getting her husband a retrial, claiming he'd been framed. No one in the office that day had wanted to hear what Becca had to say, especially because it pertained to Charlottesville's finest men in blue. But for some reason, Carson had been intrigued and had invited Becca to a nearby café for coffee.

Although she'd had to admit Becca's story had sounded farfetched, Carson had checked things out and found some plausible truth in her claim. When she'd taken it to her boss and asked for an okay to investigate Becca's allegations, he'd given it to her.

It had taken Carson almost a full year to build her case and during that time, she and Becca had become close friends. So every year since Roland's release, she would join him on Becca's birthday to celebrate the life of a woman who'd lost her life, trying to clear her husband of crime he hadn't committed. Roland had loved Becca something fierce and had taken her death hard. They both had. As a result, their friendship had grown over the years.

Considering the six-year difference in their ages, she considered Roland the younger brother she never had. She often wondered if Roland would ever remarry. The one time she'd asked him, he'd told her that he was destined to love only one woman in his life time and that woman had been Becca. Now he was married to the Summers Security Firm, the bodyguard company he'd opened up a few years ago.

Pasting a bright smile on her face, she moved toward the table where Roland sat. "Sorry if I kept you waiting, Roland."

He glanced up and it almost hurt to look at him. She could clearly see the pain in his eyes. He smiled anyway when he saw her and stood up to pull out her chair. "No problem. I haven't been waiting long."

She intended to try and cheer him up. The one way she knew she could do that was to talk about Becca. She could and would not ignore the reason they had met here tonight. "Glad you picked this place," she said, glancing around. "I came here once with Becca. God, she loved Italian food."

Roland chuckled. "Yes, she did. I recalled her first attempt at making lasagna. It was a total flop but I ate it anyway."

They burst out laughing and started regaling each other with Becca stories. It was always good talking about Becca Summers and what a truly wonderful person she was. The waiter came and took their dinner order and in memory of Becca, they both asked for lasagna.

"So how are things going with Summers Security Firm?" she asked him.

"Great. We're taking on new clients so I'm looking for able-bodied men to hire."

"Experienced?"

"Not necessary. I'm still working with that tactical training school out west to train my guys."

She knew that Roland currently had six guys in his employ. She'd met most of them at one time or another. Nice guys. Hardworking. Dedicated and loyal. Three of them were ex-cons like Roland. Although they'd been at the same prison, Glenworth Penitentiary, he hadn't known them yet. Since Roland had been a cop, he'd been housed in a different building and their paths had never crossed.

"How's Roddran and the baby?"

A smile touched her lips. "Wonderful. I dropped by their place last night to see them. Myles took some time off work to help out and they looked so happy. They named the baby Zina, after Myles's grandmother."

Roland nodded. "So what's going on with you, Carson?"

Her smile widened. "Nothing much, really." Roland was someone she could talk to, so she decided to tell him the truth. "I met someone."

He lifted a brow. "Is it serious?"

She shook her head. "No." There was no way she could let it be. The emotions Sheppard Granger stirred up inside her were nothing more than an early mid-life crisis.

"You want to talk about him?"

She shook her head. "No need. Like I said, it's not serious."

"Have the two of you gone out on a date yet?"

As much as she'd like to, there was no way that could happen. At least, not for at least eight years. "No, and we won't." She paused a moment. "As to what else is going on with me, I've been keeping busy. Mostly at Delvers, working with some young inmates."

In recognition of Becca's birthday, they ordered a slice of Becca's favorite dessert--key lime pie with a scoop of vanilla ice cream. When the waiter re-filled their wine glasses, they raised their glasses in a toast.

"To Becca. Happy birthday, my friend," Carson said.

Roland smiled. "Yes. To Becca, my heart. Happy birthday," Roland said in a choked voice.

Clinking their glasses, they then took a sip of wine. It was her hope that one day Roland would meet someone who would remove the sadness from his eyes. She knew that was what Becca would have wanted.

#

"Sorry Marshall, I don't recognize any of these names." The man had a list of eight--six males and two females. Unfortunately, none of them meant anything to Sheppard. "Are they people that I'm supposed to know?"

Marshall closed his folder. "Their names came up in my investigation."

Sheppard lifted a brow. "In what way?"

"For now, I rather not say," Marshall said, standing.

Sheppard wasn't sure if the P.I. was being tight-lipped because Ambrose was in the room listening or because he wasn't ready to tell him about any new development yet.

"Thanks for taking the time to see me, Sheppard."

Sheppard stood as well. "No problem."

"Your father is out of town on a business trip, right?"

"Yes."

"When do you expect him back?"

"The end of next week."

The man merely nodded, but Sheppard could almost see the wheels turning in his head. "I'll contact him when he returns."

Sheppard wondered if the man was on to something, and if so, what? But he wasn't going to find out anything more today. Sheppard would just have to wait until his father returned to discover what was going on.

Once Ambrose escorted Marshall out, Sheppard sat back down at the table. He didn't want to build up his hopes, but if Imerson was on to something, something that could get him his freedom, maybe a future with Carson wasn't such a farfetched dream after all.

He shook his head, knowing he couldn't get his hopes up about anything. Besides, even if that were to happen and he got his freedom, there was still something that stood in his way of ever developing a relationship with her, even if she was open to the idea. That was the ten-year difference in their ages.

Granted he wasn't old enough to be her father or even a doting uncle. But still, she was in her thirties and he had sons in their twenties. Hell, he shouldn't even be attracted to her, let alone dreaming about her at night.

The intimate part of his marriage had ended long before he'd found out his wife was being unfaithful. Yet, not once during the seventeen years of his marriage had he ever strayed. He'd always given Sylvia the respect she deserved as the mother of his sons.

Sheppard glanced over to the clock on the wall. It was late afternoon and he couldn't help wondering what Carson was doing? Was she still at work? At home? And why did he care? Bottom line was that he did care, although he wished he didn't.

He stood and decided to go to the library and check his email when Ambrose returned. More than anything, he needed to keep his mind busy.

5

"Y"ou okay Sheppard?"

Sheppard stopped pacing and glanced over at Ambrose. "Yes, I'm fine." Really, he wasn't. He had been unable to sleep most of the night anticipating this meeting with Carson. He had been disappointed when she'd cancelled the meeting last week, sending word that a case she was working on needed her undivided attention, and that she would meet with him in the three weeks as originally planned. He'd wondered if the cancellation had been intentional.

"It's early. She'll be here."

He stopped pacing. "Am I that obvious, Ambrose?"

Ambrose chuckled. "Pretty much."

Instead of saying anything, Sheppard continued pacing and every so often, he would glance up at the clock. Damn, he was too old for this. He hadn't been this impatient to see a woman in years. A man who was looking fifty in the face in a few years should have a bit more self-control.

"Pretty soon you're going to have to admit to some things, Sheppard."

There was no need to ask Ambrose what those things were. Over the last few months, he'd discovered Ambrose was very observant. Very little went on that the man didn't see.

Suddenly the door opened and there she was. He stood, transfixed in place. "Hello gentlemen."

Sheppard heard Ambrose return the greeting but all he could do was stare as if it had been three years instead of three weeks since he'd last seen her. As if ignoring the fact he hadn't said a word, she moved to the table and placed her briefcase on top of it. "Let's get started, Sheppard."

He still didn't move. She glanced over at him and then suddenly became still as well. They just stood there, staring at each other, forgetting Ambrose was in the room until he cleared his throat. They both glanced over at him. "There are a few things I need to take care of. If you don't have a problem being alone with Sheppard Granger, Attorney Boyett, I will do them now."

Sheppard blinked. He knew the rules, even if Ambrose was conveniently forgetting. An inmate could not be left alone with a visitor unless it was during attorney-client consultations.

"No, I don't have a problem with it."

"Fine." And then as if to give them a heads-up, he said. "I will knock when I return." And then he opened the door and left, closing it behind him.

Carson swung her gaze back to Sheppard and stared at him. "He's not supposed to leave us alone."

Sheppard drew in a deep breath and said, "No, he's not. I guess he's bending the rules." Sheppard walked over to where Carson stood. "Maybe we should, too."

#

Carson saw the desire in Sheppard's eyes when he came to stop in front of her. How was she supposed to fight this? He stepped closer and she felt heat emitting from him and it nearly scorched her skin.

She tried to get control of the situation. More than anything, she needed to fight this. Resist the temptation. Ignore the intense attraction. Wasn't that the reason she had cancelled last week's meeting? Because she'd known she was too weak to resist?

"Sheppard? Is something wrong?"

He didn't say anything for a minute. "You cancelled the meeting last week."

From his quiet tone, she couldn't tell if it was a statement, a question or an accusation. She swallowed. "Yes, I thought it would be for the best." There was no reason to lie to him, or play any unnecessary games. It was what it was. Lust was ruling whatever time they spent together and they both knew it.

"I thought so too," he said. "But…"

She swallowed. "But what?"

"But that was before this morning, when I woke up with a need to see you. Can we be honest about something Carson?"

"About what?"

"That this thing between us shouldn't be happening."

Though she agreed with him, she wondered at his reasoning. "Why not?"

If her question surprised him, he didn't show it. "I can give you a number of reasons. First and foremost, I'm a lot older than you."

Carson rolled her eyes. He wanted to play the age card but she refused to let him. "Ten years. Big deal."

"How did you know it's a ten year difference?"

Her gaze flickered warily. How would he handle knowing she had done research on him? She was about to find out. "I looked you up on online."

Silence as thick as mud oozed between them and she couldn't decipher his expression. Then he finally asked, "Did you find out everything you wanted to know?"

He didn't sound upset about it. "No, I didn't find out everything."

"So what else do you want to know about me?"

Was she imagining it or had he moved closer? "You were charged with murder. Did you do it?"

#

Sheppard ignored the twist in his gut at her question. Anyone who truly knew him would not have asked. But that was just it. She didn't know him and more than anything, against his better judgement, he wanted her to know him. He wanted her to believe that he could not have done what he was locked up for.

"No. I did not kill my wife."

"That means…"

She trailed off her words but he knew what she was about to say. "That means the real killer is still out there." He didn't want to discuss things he couldn't change. Just like he couldn't get his hopes up that Marshall Imerson was on to something that could possibly procure his freedom.

He took a step back. Maybe it was a good thing her question had come when it had, effectively dousing water on a fire that had almost gotten out of control. There was no way anything could ever develop between them. Over the past month or so, he had allowed himself to dream. It was time to deal with reality. Time to handle the nature of the business they were meeting for today.

He took another step back, away from temptation, away from her. He glanced at her briefcase. She had yet to take any files out. "So what do you have for me today?"

A part of Carson refused to let the moment they'd come close to sharing be lost. She figured there would be implications with asking her question, but what she hadn't counted on was the immediate distance he put between them. She wasn't sure what was causing thoughts of rebellion to flow in her head. All she knew was at that moment, she refused to let Sheppard decide their fate.

Against her better judgement, instead of opening her briefcase and pulling out the files, she stepped forward, recovering the distance separating them. The moment she did so, the frissons of fire that burned between them flared all over again. "We still need to talk about this thing between us, Sheppard."

He was looking at her in a way that made her acutely aware of his male power and strength. It made her ache for his touch. "We've done that. Like I said, the difference in our ages tops the list," he said. She saw his gaze dip from her eyes to her mouth. He began studying it with an intensity that nearly made her groan.

"Maybe it heads your list, but not mine." She took a step even closer. "No matter what reasons you've come up with, it really doesn't matter."

He lifted a brow. "Why not?"

She knew she shouldn't say what she was thinking, but something compelled her to do so anyway. "Because at this very moment, what I want more than anything is for you to kiss me."

#

Sheppard dropped his hands to his sides, as if caught off guard by Carson's request. The desire between them was palpable and he needed the kiss as much as she did. But...

He knew kissing her would be a major game changer. He would be crossing over into forbidden territory. Getting involved in something that he didn't want to be involved in. He drew in a deep breath. That was a lie. He did want to be involved. He had been pushed to the limit. He could no longer hold back, could no longer deny himself something he wanted. Something that he, at that moment, truly needed. Before he could talk himself out of doing it, he reached out and pulled her into his arms.

The moment their lips touched, powerful shivers raced down Sheppard's spine. He wanted to fill her mind, senses, her entire being with his taste. The same way she was filling him with hers.

Their tongues mingled, tangled and devoured. Nothing escaped their ravenous hunger and for the first time in over ten years, he knew how it felt to want a woman to the point where your mind became void of rules, regulations and just plain decency. The only thing consuming his thoughts was the woman he was holding in his arms. The woman he was kissing as if she was the one his mouth had been made for.

This is what he'd dreamed of doing over the past few months and now his primal instincts were kicking in with a vengeance. Something about this kiss soothed him one minute and overwhelmed him the next. A sense of urgency had him using his tongue to gobble up every inch of her mouth, from corner to corner. And when he heard her moan, he deepened the kiss, wanting and needing to taste her as much as he wanted her to taste him.

Wrapping his arms around her waist, he brought her body closer to his as he continued to take everything she was offering, kissing her like there was no tomorrow, like this might be his last opportunity. Stolen kisses. Hijacked moments. Forbidden needs. Dangerous wants and desires.

Today he was being consumed by them all and was too weak to deny himself anything. He blamed it on her unique taste. A succulent blend of woman and passion. He felt his erection harden even more as it pressed against her middle. His senses were soaring. Awareness intensified. The air surrounding them appeared electrified.

Blood was rushing through his veins, driving him toward a fine edge of lusty craziness. Sensations continued to swamp his body, overtaking his sanity. And when she shifted her body to meld it even closer to his, making his erection poke deeply against her, he tightened his arms around her waist. His better judgement was being replaced by a sensuality so urgent and sharp, everywhere he placed his tongue inside her mouth sizzled.

She pulled her mouth away from his, snatching air into her lungs. And as if a moment of weakness consumed her, she wrapped her arms around his neck while resting her forehead against his.

It took a while for them to get their breathing back under control and then she pulled back slightly and looked at him, holding his gaze. "I needed that, Sheppard."

Logic was returning two-fold and as he licked his lips, enjoying the taste of her lingering there, he knew he had to put a stop to this madness before it could go any further. "Carson, we can't--"

She quickly pressed a finger to his lips. "I don't want to hear the negatives, Sheppard. Just the positives."

Positives? He shook his head. "I'm afraid there aren't any positives. Besides the ten-year age difference, I have twenty more years in this place. I have nothing to offer you."

A smile touched her lips, lips that were still damp from their kiss. "You do, and you have already. Today you offered yourself. And I took it."

#

Later that night Carson sat cross-legged in the middle of her bed working on her laptop, typing in notes on an important case; one that was headed to trial. A woman was accused of shoplifting at a department store and accosted by store security upon leaving. She'd been literally tackled to the ground and in the process, her head had been banged up and her arm, broken. When no merchandise was found on the woman, the store gave her an apology and offered to pay her medical bills. However, since this particular department store was notorious for falsely accusing people of shoplifting, Carson's client decided to make a point and sue the store. So far, no acceptable settlement had been reached.

She then thought about the good news she'd received earlier that day. Judge Witherspoon had agreed that the charges against Craig Long should be dropped. His family had been ecstatic and couldn't wait to bring their son home. She was happy, as well. It had been proven that another man had broken into the ski shop. The police had pulled Craig over when his car matched the description of the robber's. He'd been taken down to police headquarters and forced to confess to the crime under duress and intimidation.

Carson had been the one to drive out to Delvers for the second time that day to deliver the news to Craig herself. He'd cried tears of happiness at the thought of being free after a full year of incarceration.

Her thoughts shifted to Sheppard and she allowed herself to relive those moments earlier today with him. No further discussion about their kiss could be made when a knock on the door had signaled Ambrose's return.

As if Ambrose hadn't a clue about what they'd been up to in his absence, he'd gone to his spot in the corner and pulled out his crossword puzzle. She and Sheppard didn't have any choice but to keep the overpowering sexual chemistry between them at bay.

She had to give him credit for trying and would give herself a pat on the back as well. But still, the irresistible sensual pull between them kept getting in the way, resulting in stolen glances, brushing of their hands when they exchanged papers, breathing on each other. She had become aroused just from his scent. And when she'd intentionally brushed her leg against his, he'd sucked in a sharp breath and glanced over at her. She was certain the guilty look on her face let him know the move had been intentional.

Even when he'd apprised her of the situation with Matthew Fontane, which was definitely a serious subject, she had watched his mouth move, had listened to the sound of his voice, had heard the even tempo of his breathing and had gotten turned on by all three. By the time the meeting ended, she'd worked up more sexual frustration in that one hour than she had in all the years since Pence.

Just thinking about the kiss they'd shared brought desire rushing through her body. She knew Sheppard would dominate her dreams tonight, just as he had the last few. But this time, it would be different. Now she knew his taste, and it was something she couldn't forget.

#

Sheppard couldn't sleep. He just couldn't get that kiss out of his mind. It was the first time he'd kissed a woman in more than ten years and he'd enjoyed it. Too much. He'd reached the point where he hadn't wanted to stop and probably could have gone even longer if she hadn't needed to come up for air.

He'd heard from Ambrose that Carson had returned to Delvers that evening to deliver some good news to Craig Long. A judge had overturned his conviction and Craig would be leaving Delvers soon. Sheppard was happy for the young man and was glad about Carson's victory.

Everything about her had broken down his resolve today and that kiss had basically been the turning point. He'd tried to get her to see that there could not be anything between them. Why start something they couldn't finish? Carson was more than a steal-a-kiss-every-now-and-then-woman. She deserved more. She deserved to have a man sleeping beside her each night. A man who could hold her whenever she needed to be held. A man who could take her out to dinner then out for a night out on the town. A man who could do things with her every weekend.

As much as he wished otherwise, he was not that man. There were too many minuses. Too few pluses. He no longer wore tailor made suits. His most popular outfit only came in the color orange and with one design. He couldn't sleep with her, share a meal with her or take her any place outside these barricaded walls. So why was he letting her get to him in a way no other women ever had? Why was he already counting the days when he would see her again? And why was he allowing her to create a need inside of him that could never be quenched?

As a businessman, he knew the pitfalls, the blatant risks of going after something you knew wasn't feasible to acquire. Somehow he had to make her understand. Because if he ever kissed her again, another chunk would fall from his shield of armor.

When he saw her again, he would make things absolutely clear that there was no way anything could get started between them. It was a waste of time and energy. A no-win situation.

He had to do this. He would do this. It was for the best.

6

Carson smiled as she walked beside her client as they left the judge's chamber. Ingrid Adelson's smile was even larger, understandably so. They had asked for seven million and settled on five. The opposing counsel had tried playing hardball, claiming they would not offer any more than two and had threatened to take it to court. Carson knew their threat was a bluff, especially since this particular case was getting a lot of national attention in the media. It was a case of David against Goliath and they wouldn't want a jury to decide the outcome. Especially since there was a chance the judge might allow Perriman Department Store's history to be considered; namely, how often their store security had violated human rights.

"So what's next for you?" she asked Ingrid as they walked out the building.

"First I want to digest it all in. Then I want to set up a meeting with those charities I've selected to give some of the money to."

Carson had seen the list. The American Cancer Society topped it and she understood. Both of Ingrid's parents had died of cancer within a year of each other. "Good idea."

Ingrid glanced over at her. "You were super in there. Those other attorneys really tried to intimidate you."

Yes, they had tried. It had been three men against one female and they figured they would make her sweat. They hadn't liked that not only had she not faltered, but her cool had been astounding. "As you can see, their tactic didn't work." Unfortunately, she performed better under pressure.

Unless that pressure involved a man name Sheppard Granger.

She tried pushing the call she'd gotten yesterday from an administrative assistant at Delvers to the back of her mind. The meeting she'd looked forward to today with Sheppard had been cancelled. No plausible reason had been given but as far as she was concerned, none was needed. He was doing the same thing to her that she had done to him weeks ago. He was running. Away from her. If that kiss they'd shared had knocked out her senses, she could only imagine what it had done to his.

She knew what his concerns were. Sheppard had said it all in the letter she'd received at her office the beginning of the week. She could remember every single word...

Attorney Boyett,

Before we meet again, I believe that we need to agree that our discussions should be kept on the strictest professional level. As much as I wish otherwise, the difference in our ages prohibits anything personal from developing between us. That, and the fact that I am a

*convict, makes a relationship impossible. You have a lot to
offer a man. Don't waste it on someone who has nothing.*
Respectfully,
Sheppard M. Granger

When she'd first read the letter, she'd been upset--not
at Sheppard but at the situation that had locked an innocent
man up behind bars. The attorney in her couldn't blame the
judicial system or the jury who'd found him guilty. She
was placing the blame solely at the feet of his attorney.

Over the past couple of weeks, she had read transcripts
from his trial. She wasn't someone who would normally
critique a fellow attorney's handling of a case, but there
had been so many missed opportunities during Sheppard's
hearing, she often wondered if his attorney had been
working for him or for the prosecution. Sheppard was a
smart man. Surely he knew of his attorney's incompetence.
So why hadn't he replaced the man?

"Will you celebrate tonight?" Ingrid asked.

She glanced over at her. Deciding not to give her client
a glimpse into her dull and boring life, she said, "That's my
plan."

There was no need to explain that later tonight all she
planned to do was go home and enjoy a glass of wine. Her
reasons would be two-fold--to indulge in the thrill of
victory, as well as to sit back and reflect upon regrets. More
than anything, she had wanted to see Sheppard today, if for

no other reason than to joyfully share a moment in his presence.

She tried not to let disappointment overwhelm her, but found it difficult. She doubted her response to his letter would sway him to consider the stand he was taking. Her short reply had simply said...

Sheppard,

While I don't have a problem keeping our meetings on a professional level, I don't agree with the rest.

Carson

She could only surmise that his cancelling of today's meeting was his way of letting her know that he hadn't particularly liked what she'd written. Oh, well. They would eventually see each other again, that was a given. She would be patient and let him resolve any inner turmoil he was dealing with.

Carson was convinced that there was something different, something monumental, going on between them. There was no other explanation for the intense attraction they shared. She'd never been an aggressive female when it came to men. However, she knew if she gave Sheppard the opportunity to retreat, he would take it. And she couldn't let him do that.

#

"You okay Shep? You seem pretty distracted today."

Sheppard glanced over at his father and saw the concerned look in the older man's gaze. Richard Granger was the one man Sheppard had always admired. There had never been a time he hadn't wanted to follow in his father's footsteps, to learn so much from him. To constantly make him proud. His father had never demanded anything of him, other than to do his best. He'd married the woman his mother had deemed the perfect wife, although he'd known his father had had his misgivings. However, Richard had not interfered or stated how he truly felt. A part of Sheppard wished that he had.

He drew in a deep breath. There was no need to tell his father about Carson, how hard he'd been trying to distance himself from her when deep down, all he wanted to do was see her again. He hadn't known not seeing her would make him this miserable. More miserable than he'd been in a long time. Even Ambrose had asked him what was wrong.

"I'm fine Dad. I just have a lot on my mind." He quickly decided to change the subject before his father inquired as to what some of those things were. "And you still haven't heard any more from Marshall?"

Richard shook his head. "No, not since a couple of weeks ago. When I returned from Puerto Rico, he called and said he was on to something big but couldn't go into any details."

Sheppard nodded. Marshall had alluded to the same thing to him when he'd visited, and Sheppard had been thinking hard as to what he could have uncovered. He studied his father. Was he imagining things or did the old man look more relaxed than he had the last time he'd seen him? Sheppard didn't see the usual strain that often lined his father's features whenever he visited.

"You're looking well, Dad. That business trip to Puerto Rico must have been pretty relaxing." Was he imagining things, or did his father just blush.

"Yes, it was rather relaxing."

He had a feeling his father wanted to say more and knew it wasn't Ambrose's presence that was stopping him. As usual, the prison guard was engrossed in his crossword puzzle. Besides, over the last several months, he knew his father had gotten used to Ambrose and liked him a lot. Being able to meet with his father face-to-face in a private room was a lot nicer than having a glass partition between them. He figured he had Ambrose to thank for that, too.

"Is there something going on that I should know about?" Sheppard finally asked, picking up on Richard's nervousness.

His father met his gaze. "I'm dating."

Sheppard blinked. That hadn't been what he expected to hear. As far as he knew, Richard hadn't dated since his mother's death. Ava Marie Granger had died more than twenty years ago and everyone had taken her death hard. She had been the epitome of a loving and gracious wife, perfect for her husband in every way. They had been partners in all things. He knew losing a baby within days of his birth had been hard on them--although at four Sheppard had been too young to fully understand--but they'd weathered the storm and he thought the loss had brought them even closer.

"I'm glad, Dad. Honestly, I am happy for you. Mom's been gone for a long time and you've buried yourself in work for too long. If things had worked out differently, you would have been retired by now."

A wry smile touched his father's lips. "From Granger Aeronautics, yes, but not from work. I probably would be more involved in that foundation I established for your mother."

Sheppard nodded. He knew the Ava Granger Foundation was still doing great charity work in Charlottesville. One of the first things the foundation had done was to build the Ava Granger Wing at St. Francis Memorial Hospital.

"So Dad, who's the lucky lady?"

Richard paused a minute and Sheppard watched the deep coloring return to his cheeks.

"The lady I am serious about, Shep, is Hannah."

Sheppard knew his face had to radiate his shock. "*My* Hannah?"

Richard smiled and nodded. "Yes, *your* Hannah. *Our* Hannah."

Hannah had been the Granger's housekeeper for years, but before that, she'd been hired as Sheppard's nanny. He couldn't remember a time when she hadn't been an important part of his life. She'd taken over as head housekeeper before Sheppard had married and had been there to help him raise his sons. Jace, Caden and Dalton all adored her and she loved them.

Hannah wasn't considered an employee but a member of the Granger family. She was someone he knew his father trusted implicitly. She was someone he could talk to and confide in. He figured the place had to have gotten pretty lonely after the boys moved away for school. Both Richard and Hannah had lost their beloved spouses, so Sheppard could understand them coming together.

Hannah visited him at least once a month and he'd always complimented her on how good she looked for a woman in her sixties. Hannah was a beautiful woman. And his father was a good looking man in his early seventies. It made a lot of sense.

But still…

He just couldn't imagine the fun-loving Hannah and the ultra-conservative Richard Granger as a couple. "Did you take Hannah to Puerto Rico with you?"

"Yes. I've been trying to get her to go out of town with me for a while. We're keeping our relationship a secret, for now. It was Hannah's decision, not mine. I told her I would give her whatever she wanted, as long as we could be together." He paused a minute. "I love her Shep and she loves me. And in case you're wondering if there was ever anything between us when your mother was alive, there wasn't."

Sheppard drew in a deep breath. "I know that, Dad. Mom's been dead over twenty years. I'm sure it's been lonely for you."

"Yes, but I had you and the boys. And when you left, the boys kept me busy...and on my toes. There was never a dull moment with that Dalton."

Sheppard heard the fondness in his voice. For his father, Dalton may have been the most challenging of Shep's three sons, but the love was there in his tone regardless. "I'm hoping that one day Hannah will feel comfortable about bringing our love out in the open," Richard said.

Sheppard smiled. "I hope so, too. The two of you deserve to be happy. You know how I feel about Hannah."

"Yes, I know and she loves you and the boys just as much."

Sheppard didn't say anything for a minute. "Dad, can I ask you something?"

"You can ask me anything, son."

Sheppard leaned forward and rested his arms on his thighs. "I know Hannah is six years younger than you. The difference in your ages doesn't bother you?"

Richard shook his head. "No, not at all."

"What if there was a ten-year difference?"

"It still wouldn't bother me. I've discovered age doesn't matter when you care deeply for someone. Since your mother's death, I've been approached by a number of women, young and old, claiming interest. Some were young enough to be my daughter or granddaughter. They might have been interested, but I wasn't. What really interested them was the Granger's wealth. I'm not a stupid man. I know when a woman is sincere and when she is not."

Sheppard nodded. Yes, his father would know. Although his father thought an age difference was no big deal, Sheppard still had that even bigger stumbling block to get past—he was a man in prison. And he still contended that Carson Boyett deserved better than that.

7

Carson had gotten a call first thing this morning from Delvers. Sheppard Granger had requested to meet with her. So here she was, ten minutes before the hour, wondering what this meeting was about. Had Matthew Fontane gotten into more trouble or was this a rescheduling of the meeting Sheppard had cancelled a couple of weeks ago? Warden Smallwood's personal assistant hadn't said. Either way, she was here. She looked forward to seeing Sheppard again. He'd had a birthday last week and she'd sent him a card. She'd thought about him a lot and purposely kept herself busy, so she didn't go crazy.

Since her victory with Ingrid's case, she'd taken on new clients, grateful for the opportunity to build up her firm. She was even thinking about bringing in another attorney, the way her workload was growing. Right now, she was able to handle what she had and still dedicate some time to her pro bono work.

She had visited with Roddran, Myles and the baby yesterday. They had broken the news to her that Myles had accepted a job offer in Texas and they would be moving there in a couple of months. Although she knew this would be a huge promotion for Myles, a chance to become partner in a prestigious law firm, she hated to see her best friend leave Charlottesville. But she knew Houston was just a flight away and she would make it her business to visit often. Especially since she had agreed to become godmother to Zina. The christening ceremony was to take place this coming Sunday.

Yesterday, she had lunch with Roland at his office and had seen several of his employees she'd met a few months ago; three bodyguards who had once been inmates at Glenworth. Though she knew Glenworth was a huge facility, she asked if they'd met Sheppard while confined there. They had. Furthermore, the three said Sheppard had been their mentor, a role model, someone they could look up to, someone who'd always had their backs. By the end of the conversation, she gathered Sheppard was someone they highly respected.

Carson really wasn't surprised. Just being around him had shown her just what a decent man he was. Any woman would appreciate having someone like him in her life. She definitely would.

Getting out of her car at the prison, she pulled her entry badge from her purse. As she walked toward the guarded entrance, she tried keeping her heart from pounding in her chest.

\#

Sheppard stood at the library window and watched as Carson got out of her car. The moment he set eyes on her, he'd felt a pull in his gut. As usual, she was dressed in a business suit. This one was royal blue. She dressed for success and the businessman in him liked that. As she walked toward the building, he couldn't help noticing the way her hips swayed with every step she took.

Carson Boyett was a beautiful woman. An irresistible woman.

And more than anything, she was an unforgettable woman.

Lord knew, he'd tried forgetting her by putting distance between them. That hadn't worked. He'd finally come to terms with the fact that he couldn't hold out not seeing her any longer. He thought of her every single day and dreamed about her each night. And when he'd gotten that birthday card from her last week, he'd been deeply touched. He hadn't realized she'd known his birthdate. The card had even smelled like her and he'd wondered if she'd sprayed it with her perfume. Convinced she had, he'd slept with the card beneath his pillow each night, closing his eyes to her scent.

He kept looking out the window and watching for her until she'd arrived. It was then that his thoughts shifted to all the other birthday greetings he'd received--emails, cards and calls. The emails had mostly come from the young men he'd mentored while at Glenworth, as well as others employees at Granger Aeronautics. He was touched they had remembered his birthday. Hannah had called and so had his dad.

He'd gotten several hand-made cards from every guy on his team except for Fontane. Sheppard suspected Fontane was still in a bad mood--a lot of his privileges had been taken away for six months. As far as Sheppard was concerned, Fontane had brought it on himself.

All three of his sons had called and it had been great talking to them. They were doing fine and were making plans to see him in a few months. Although he much preferred seeing them together, he knew their visits would be at different times. Jace and Caden had visited him together at Christmas, but not Dalton. His youngest son had visited him a couple months later. Sheppard had a feeling Jace and Caden were upset with their younger brother about something, but neither had elaborated.

He heard the knock on the media room door seconds before Ambrose entered. "Attorney Boyett has arrived."

#

"Good afternoon gentlemen," Carson said, walking into the room. Both men stood when she entered and returned her greeting.

She tried keeping her gaze from lingering on Sheppard. Still, that was all it took, a handful of seconds to take in all of him. Was her mind playing tricks on her? Was Sheppard more handsome today than he'd been when she'd seen him last?

Carson placed her briefcase on the table and, out of the corner of her eye, saw Sheppard sit back down. "I need to make an important phone call," Ambrose said, heading for the door.

When the door closed, she began pulling folders out of her briefcase. Although she didn't know why Sheppard had wanted to see her, the timing had worked since she needed to apprise him of something.

"Congratulations on getting Craig's conviction overturned," Sheppard said.

She smiled. "Thanks." Then her smile was replaced with a frown. "I got some bad news, Sheppard. I've already told Warden Smallwood."

Their eyes met and held way too long. "What?"

Noticing the tense lines of his lips only reminded her of the taste of those lips. His entire mouth. "It's about Matthew Fontane."

"What about Matthew?"

"The parole board has removed his name from consideration."

Sheppard drew in a deep breath and patted the top of his head. "I figured they would after the stunt he pulled last month. When will he be eligible again?"

"He won't be."

The room got silent and she knew why. What she'd said meant Fontane would be serving all five years of his sentence without any chance of parole. "He brought this on himself, Sheppard," she said.

"I know," he said in a low tone.

Carson heard the disappointment in his voice and understood. A number of the young men he mentored had gotten their sentences reduced due to positive changes he'd helped make in their lives. He took that role seriously and had turned around even some of the hardest young criminals, convincing them they had more to offer society than a life of crime. Some of them never had a positive male influence in their lives until Sheppard. Because he believed in them, they began believing in themselves.

"You did all you could. You can't blame yourself that Fontane wasn't cooperative. His failure to accept the reason he's at Delvers continues to be his downfall," she said, fighting the urge to go to him and wrap her arms around him.

He leaned back in the chair and she watched the movement, thinking something as casual as that could increase her heart rate. Apparently he'd decided to sit farther away from her than he had at previous meetings. That didn't bother her since she was able to see more of him. Her gaze soaked him up…especially how his orange trousers stretched across a pair of muscular thighs. Even dressed in prison orange, Sheppard Granger stood out. His charismatic nature was like a magnet. It was what continued to draw her to him.

Forcing her attention away from him and back to the business at hand, she said. "And there's something else."

"What?" he asked.

She glanced back over at him and blood raced through her veins. The beauty of his dark eyes, as well as the perfect symmetry of his angular jaw were such a turn-on. "He'll receive annual evaluations. If he continues to cause problems, additional time will be added. Every incident, no matter how minor, will add years to his sentence."

Sheppard didn't say anything. Then as she watched, seemingly in one fluid motion, he stood and began pacing with his hands deep into his pockets. Her pulse kicked up a few notches. There was nothing like seeing the body of a well-built man in motion. Although troubled, his steps were smooth, suave and sexy. And his shoulders--broad and muscular--finally shrugged in resignation.

He stopped pacing and glanced over at her. "Fontane won't handle that news well." He paused a moment. "I've got to get through to him."

Carson heard determination in his voice. She knew if anyone could get through to Matthew Fontane, it would be Sheppard. "And you will."

"Thanks for the vote of confidence."

Sexual chemistry which had been simmering around them from the moment she'd walked into the room, was flaring up to the boiling point and she couldn't let that happen. Otherwise, she would be tempted to rush across the room and throw herself in his arms, begging to be kissed. The thought of him sliding his tongue inside her mouth stroked sensations within her.

Trying to ignore the sexual energy stirring the air, she said. "By the way, I recently ran into three young men I believe you know."

He came back to the table and sat down. His masculine body appeared convulsed in erotic undercurrents. "Oh? Who?"

"Striker Jennings, Quasar Patterson and Stonewall Courson."

His lips curved into a smile and she noticed a lushness about his entire mouth, especially his bottom lip. "Yes. I know them very well. How did you meet them?" Sheppard asked.

"They work as bodyguards for a friend of mine."

Sheppard lifted a brow. "You're a friend of the owner of Summers Security Firm?"

She smiled. "Yes, Roland Summers and I have known each other for years." A smile touched her lips. "I stopped by his office last week and the three guys were there. I met them a while back but this was the first time we've held any kind of conversation. Imagine my surprise when they mentioned they knew you. Small world."

"Yes, small world."

Sheppard tried ignoring the dash of jealousy that raced through him. He had no problem calling the emotion what it was, although he had no right to be jealous when it came to her. But he couldn't help it. Although he'd never officially met Roland Summers, he'd heard a lot of good things about him from Striker, Quasar and Stonewall. They often said what a great guy their boss was. They'd also shared that he was a widower in his thirties.

And Carson was a divorcee also in her thirties.

Sheppard couldn't help wondering how close she was to Roland. Were they dating? Lovers? It really wasn't any of his business one way or the other. However, he wanted to know.

"Was there a reason you wanted to see me today, Sheppard?"

Yes, there was a reason, but first he wanted her to explain the nature of her relationship with Roland Summers. Instead of answering her question, he had one of his own.

"You and Roland Summers?"

She lifted a brow. "Yes? What about us?"

"Sounds like the two of you are close."

"We are."

His throat constricted as disappointment settled in his lungs. "Yet, you've let me kiss you."

It suddenly dawned on Carson what Sheppard was thinking. "Yes, I let you kiss me because my relationship with Roland isn't like that. He's six years younger and I consider him the brother I always wanted, but never had."

She closed her file, wanting to make sure he fully understood. "I was friends with Roland's wife Becca before I met Roland. He was a cop serving time, framed by a bunch of fellow bad cops and she wanted me to prove his innocence and get him released."

Sheppard didn't say anything for a minute. "You did get him out but not before his wife was murdered," he said, as if he'd heard the narrative from somewhere. Or maybe he'd researched her on internet, the way she'd done him.

"Yes. Roland took her death pretty hard. We both did. Becca had become a good friend. Now he's a good friend."

She didn't say anything for a minute and then said, "I hope you don't think I could kiss you and be involved with another guy."

Sheppard tilted his head back, wanting to see her fully. At that moment, he knew the answer. No, he didn't think that. He also knew something else. He wanted to kiss her. He *had* to kiss her again.

Easing out of his chair, he took the few steps to where she sat staring up at him. "To be honest Carson, whenever I'm around you, it's hard for me to think at all. My mind is too busy wanting you. I see you and I want you. I smell you and I want you. We touch and I want you. I can't think for wanting you, Carson."

He heard the ragged breath flowing past her lips. God, she breathed and he wanted her. "The reason I asked you to come here today is because I had to see you again. I tried, but I can't fight wanting you any longer, although I know I should. Even when I know wanting you will get me nowhere. I have nothing to offer you."

She shook her head. "Please let's not go back to that again."

"It should not have been taken off the table, Carson. After our last meeting, I'd pretty much reached some firm conclusions."

"Such as?"

"Such as when I saw you again, I intended to make things absolutely clear that there's no way anything could get started between us. It would be a waste of time and energy. A no-win situation."

She eased out of her chair to stand in front of him. "I hate to break the news to you, but things have already gotten started, and I happen to see it as a winning situation. So what if you can't take me out to dinner or show up at my place every now and then? I took myself off the dating market some time ago so…"

"Why?"

She leaned back against the table, resting her hips on the edge. His gaze followed her movements. "I don't have time to go into all the gory details. Just take my word for it."

He didn't say anything and could only reach one conclusion. "Bad first marriage?"

"The worse. Pence Denmark could teach a class on Fundamentals of Being an Asshole 101. Then there are the single men out there who think I owe them something...namely in the bedroom. Unfortunately, they found out I don't need them as much as they like to think I do. So not having you constantly underfoot won't bother me."

He wasn't quite sure what to make of that. "So what are your expectations?"

She tilted her head at an angle that showed what an attractive neck she had. It was both graceful and elegant. A smile curved her lips. "I don't have any, other than I'd like to get to know you better before I invite you over for dinner."

He chuckled. "Invite me over? Will twenty years be long enough? I might not be going anywhere until then. I can't even count on parole in eight."

She shrugged her beautiful shoulders. "Think positive, Sheppard. I understand you have a private investigator working hard to get you out of here."

"And you heard that from whom?"

"Three men who're ready to see you more often."

He figured she was talking about Striker, Quasar and Stonewall. During one of their visits, he'd mentioned that his father had hired a top notch investigator to obtain enough evidence to submit for the reopening of his case. He hadn't mentioned anything to them about the recent developments, though. He refused to get anyone's hopes up.

"That doesn't mean anything," he stressed.

"I think that it does."

"The guy isn't the first private investigator my father has hired to get me out of here. I refuse to get my hopes up about anything and suggest no one else does either. So if you want to get to know me because you're banking on me walking out of this place a free man anytime soon, then I suggest that you don't."

She lifted her chin. "And I suggest you let me think for myself, Sheppard. But then, there could be another reason why you're so hesitant about us getting to know each other."

"What other reason is there?"

"That you don't want to get to know me as much as I want to get to know you."

Sheppard wished he could look her directly in the eyes and say that was true, that there was no point. But they'd gone through that already and she refused to let it go. And if he was honest with himself, he would admit he wanted to get to know her.

At that moment, he decided to take the road of honesty. "You're wrong Carson, I do want to get to know you. But you deserve more."

"And I've told you that--"

"I know what you've told me, but I'm afraid I'll let myself get caught up with you and start believing in possibilities that I shouldn't."

She took a step closer to him, reached out and took his hand, curling her fingers around his. He tried to ignore the spike of heat that speared though him with her touch but couldn't. "I talk to a lot of guys you've mentored here at Delvers, as well as with Striker, Quasar and Stonewall. The one thing they tell me is that, more than anything, you gave them hope. You had them believing in possibilities."

She paused a moment. "Why can't you believe in those possibilities for yourself, Sheppard? Why can't you have the same kind of hope you instill in others? That same belief that there's something better out there for you, that it's okay for you to believe that you deserve something more as much as anyone else does? You do deserve it. So take it...and take me in the process. "

Before Carson could take her next breath, Sheppard quickly leaned down and captured her mouth, immediately robbing her of her senses. Catching her tongue, he drew it into his mouth and began feasting on it with a hunger that made intense need race up her spine, settle in her mid-section before trickling between her legs.

Shudders speared through her while strength was drained from her body. Blood gushed to her head, making her feel dizzy as his tongue began mating with hers. She was filled with the taste and scent of him and couldn't get enough of either.

And she felt him, the hardness of him, pressed against her. His erection was huge and firm and only added to the intense desire building inside of her, firing a need she hadn't filled in years and reminding her she was woman who deserved to believe in possibilities as well. Along with that same hope.

She felt his hand move from her waist to take a firm grip of her hips, sitting her on the table. It was a good thing--she would have slid to the floor from the impact of the mouth mating so sensuously with hers. Only Sheppard could kiss her with such sizzling desire and ravenous passion. He was the one man who could demonstrate how much enjoyment you could derive from a kiss. He was so thorough. So painstaking methodical as he pushed her over the edge, lick by delicious lick.

Carson felt his hand move up her bare thigh, move underneath her dress and inch its way between her legs. His fingers began stroking around the material of her panties and--

They suddenly broke off the kiss and he snatched his hand from underneath her skirt when they heard conversation outside the door. Panting, Carson rested her head against Sheppard's neck, inhaling his scent and wondering if she was capable of ever breathing normal again. Then, as effortlessly as he'd placed her on the table, Sheppard eased her back on her feet. The gaze staring down at her was like a flame sucking up oxygen from the room

"You've presented a good argument, which proves what a good attorney you are," he said.

"And?" she asked, barely able to get the single word out. Just looking at his lips made her wish they could kiss again.

"And I will go along with what you suggest. That we get to know each other better."

She couldn't hold back her smile. "I think you've made the right decision, Sheppard."

"But there is one condition, Carson."

She lifted a brow. "And what condition is that?"

Carson saw resoluteness in his features and knew whatever this condition was, he would not be swayed. "Under no circumstances, no matter what opportunities are presented to us, will I *take you*. In other words, we won't go any farther than we just have. Kissing is as far as any intimacy will go between us."

She clearly understood what he was saying, but decided to ask. "Not even a quickie?"

He shook his head. "Definitely not that. I'm not proud of what I almost did to you earlier. Sitting you on that table and--"

"You didn't hear me complain," she interjected.

"Regardless, you deserve more than being made love to inside this place. I refuse to change my mind about that, Carson. So if you don't think you can accept my stipulation that we get to know each other without any real type of intimacy, then I suggest we end things between us before they begin."

She had no intention of ending anything. "Fine, we'll play by your rules, Sheppard." And then before he could think of any other conditions to tack on, she reached up and wrapped her arms around his neck, pulling his mouth down to hers in another kiss.

8

Carson stepped out on her patio to inhale the night air. It was hard to believe it was October already. Forecasters had predicted cooler weather with the days ahead and she wasn't ready for them. Leaving sunny Florida to move to Charlottesville had been hard and she doubted that she would ever get used to the sharp contrast in the temperatures.

She took a sip of her wine and looked out across her back yard. Purchasing a home instead of moving into a condo had been a decision she hadn't regretted making. While married to Pence, they had leased a condo in Tampa and more often than not, Pence would complain about the neighbor's loud music, kids putting their hand prints on his precious car or neighbors allowing their dogs to do their business near the walkway. There were constantly disagreements between him and the neighbors, and because she was married to Pence, she would get caught in the crossfire.

And then there was the embarrassment in knowing the neighbors probably knew every time she and Pence argued, since he had a tendency to throw things at her. More than once the police had been called.

Now she had her own place, with the privacy she'd always craved. Unfortunately, although she'd live here for almost six years, she didn't know her neighbors. It was mainly her fault. She could have met a number of them had she attended one of the homeowner association's potluck gatherings. But she'd always convinced herself she was either too busy or too tired.

Her thoughts drifted to Pence again. One decision she didn't regret was divorcing her ex after three years of marriage. Pence had been so mentally abusive, she often wondered why she'd stayed with him as long as she had.

Refusing to think about her ex any longer, she glanced out across her back yard. She lived in a modest community and intended to forgo the thirty-year mortgage, planning to have her house paid off in half the time. She liked the area, especially since most of the stores, shops and restaurants she frequented were just minutes away. There were several bike trails and walking paths, a community pool and recreation center. She didn't have a good view of the mountains like some of her neighbors, but her house looked out on the huge man-made lake, which she appreciated. Especially on those days when she'd come home after a hectic day at the office and needed to unwind. There was something nice about sitting on the patio in her lounger with a glass of wine, staring out over the lake. Then she could focus her thoughts on something other than work.

When she would fill her mind with thoughts of Sheppard Granger.

It had been a little over six weeks since they'd agreed to get to know each other. What Carson enjoyed about her meetings with Sheppard was that once their discussions about the young men he mentored were concluded, they would spend the rest of the time talking. Getting to know each other better. She'd told him about her divorce, the baby she'd lost, the in-laws she'd loved and why it had been hard for her to consider getting serious about any man after Pence. In turn, he'd told her about his wife and his discovery of her unfaithfulness. It appeared that his marriage had been as unhappy as hers had been. Sheppard had made the decision to remain with his wife because of his three sons.

Carson could tell he was a man who loved his children and was proud of them. He had told her he believed they knew he hadn't killed their mother.

She felt she was really getting to know him and the more she did, she saw the man Striker, Quasar and Stonewall knew and admired. The same man Warden Smallwood held in such high esteem. The same man who'd earned the respect of his fellow inmates and prison guards. He was such a strong leader, and he had the ability to understand people. He always put others before himself.

The highlight of being with Sheppard was when the meeting ended. Before she left, he would always pull her into his arms and kiss her. No matter how tempted they were to take things further, kissing was as far as they would go. She enjoyed kissing him. He had a marvelous tongue and definitely knew how to use it. And over the past weeks, he'd used it a lot on her. He always took his time when kissing her, as if he was savoring the moment.

After a Sheppard Granger kiss, she would have to hang back in the media room to recover and regain her strength. His kisses could be just that overpowering. They also had a lasting effect. She couldn't recall the number of times in between their meetings when she would lick her lips and swear she could still taste him in her mouth.

He no longer brought up the subject of their ages. Nor did he talk about the length of time he still had to be confined. Instead, she believed that he was beginning to look forward to a time when he would no longer be locked up. That was evident in the letters he'd begun writing her. She would get one every week. The letters would start off sharing his thoughts and end up stating his feelings about life in general. And about her.

Placing her wineglass on the table, she pulled out the letter she'd received that day to reread it. She'd folded it up and inserted it inside her bra, close to her heart. The contents, written in his bold, inscriptive handwriting had touched her deeply.

Carson,

I just finished dinner with a group of fine men. Most are regretting some of the choices they've made in their lives and appreciate knowing, at some point, they will be given another chance. There are some who are here because they were falsely accused of a crime they didn't commit; though there are others who haven't come around yet. They think the world owes them something. But I have hope for them.

I have retired for the night. I just finished reading my favorite book, Profiles of Courage, by John F. Kennedy. I've read it so many times over the years that the book automatically opens to my favorite parts. Now my mind is clear but before I close my eyes to sleep for the night, I decided to write you this letter.

I enjoy getting to know you and hope you enjoy getting to know me as well. The one thing I've discovered about you over the past few weeks is that you are a special woman. Words cannot explain how much you have touched my life in so many ways. I had gotten so wrapped up in mentoring others that I failed to realize that I could use some mentoring myself.

And you have mentored me in ways you don't know about. I see you and I see beauty. I see hope. I see all that's still good in the world. You light up my life in ways you will never know and I want to say thank you for making me a part of your life. I don't know our destination but I thank God so much that you picked me up for the ride. It is awesome.

Forever thinking of you,

Sheppard

Carson drew in a deep breath knowing that Sheppard had no idea how much he lit up her world as well. And she knew, at that moment, she had fallen in love with him. There was no need to wonder why her heartbeat kicked up whenever she saw him or why just sharing his space meant so much to her.

She was well aware of how a future looked for them, but she was willing to take it one day at a time because no man had touched her the way he had. No man had ever come close to making her feel irresistibly special in such a warm-hearted way. He never used lines. Instead, he spoke from his heart through a kind mouth. And then, that same mouth could arouse her in ways she hadn't thought possible.

Carson recalled the last time they'd met and how their control had been tested. Despite the boundaries Sheppard had set, it was getting harder and harder for him to keep his hands from under her skirt whenever they kissed. And she'd been equally tempted to unzip his pants a time or two. He'd caught hold of her hand to stop her more than once. She would promise to behave the next time but never did. She couldn't be blamed when he was so darn sexy and had the ability to make her want to do naughty things.

She refolded the letter and placed it back in her bosom, close to her heart. Filled with emotions she'd never felt before, her life vibrated with new meaning and a whole new direction. The thought made her smile. "I love you, Sheppard Granger," she whispered softly and with easy acceptance. One day she would say those words to him.

Happiness touched her in knowing in a few more days she would be seeing him again.

#

"Sheppard?"

He glanced up at Ambrose. "Yes?"

"I just heard that Fontane is on his way up for your meeting with him."

"Okay." Ambrose was about to walk off when Sheppard stopped him. "Wait a minute, Ambrose. There's something I need to talk to you about."

The prison guard lifted a brow. "Okay. What is it?"

"All the private time you're deliberately giving to me and Carson. You're breaking rules for us. Why?"

Ambrose didn't say anything for a long moment. Then he admitted, "I've been a prison guard for a long time Sheppard. Close to twenty years. I've had to deal with hard-core criminals and some not so hard-core, like the ones here at Delvers. But the one thing I've always tried to do is not dehumanize anyone, regardless of the reason they are locked up. Everyone has a story and it's not always the one you assume it to be."

The man then took a deep breath as he leaned against the closed door. "I'd heard about you long before you came to Delvers, Sheppard. I have associates at Glenworth who actually appreciated you being there because it made their job easier, less stressful. You gave young men hope instead of adding to their misery. You made them take ownership of the situation they were in. And you're doing the same thing here."

Ambrose shook his head slightly. "Attorney Boyett is also a good person. She doesn't have to give up her free time and come here, yet she does. I've been married a long time and I love my wife. I love my sons. I'm not stupid, nor am I insensitive. I can read people and recognized the spark between you and Attorney Boyett for what it was. I know you would never ask me to allow the two of you extra time because that's not who you are. You would worry about the consequences for me."

"Yes, I don't want you to get into any trouble," Sheppard stressed.

Ambrose nodded. "I know you don't and I won't. My job gives me the authority to make decisions about certain things and I have. Just like Warden Smallwood trusts you, I trust you as well. There aren't too many men like you, Sheppard, and I regret the course of events that brought you here. But I appreciate knowing you, watching you and even guarding you. Where you're concerned, I will continue to do my job as I see fit."

Ambrose's words had touched Sheppard. Fighting back emotions, he said, "Thank you."

"You're welcome."

There was a hard knock on the door. Ambrose motioned his head to the door. "Sounds like Fontane has arrived."

#

"I'm going to die if I stay in here any longer."

Sheppard leaned back in his chair and watched as Matthew Fontane paced around the room like a caged animal. He'd told Fontane weeks ago the decision the parole board had made and Fontane hadn't taken it well. "I've been locked up a lot longer than you Fontane and I haven't died yet," he said. In fact, he was getting a little sick of the young man's pity party. "You need to grow up, Fontane. Start taking some responsibility for your actions."

Hostile dark eyes glared at him. "You don't know how I feel."

"Yeah, right. I've been locked up in here for my health," Sheppard said. "What you need is some sense knocked into you."

Fontane stiffened his spine, as if gearing up for a fight. "Don't even try it old man."

"Trust me, I won't. What's going to happen if you don't improve your attitude is that you're going to get more time added to your sentence. That means an automatic transfer to Glenworth."

Fear suddenly flashed across Fontane's face. "I can't go there." He dropped into a chair and covered his face with his hands. "I'd die," he moaned. "They'll kill me if I go there."

Concern overcame Sheppard. "Who would kill you?"

"The guys I was with that night. The night we tried to hijack the car. They got a longer sentence and were sent to Glenworth. I've heard they are accusing me of being a traitor since I stayed behind and saved that old man."

Sheppard stood and walked over to Fontane, placing a hand on his shoulder. "It will be up to you if you end up at Glenworth. You control your future. No one else does."

Dark eyes looked up at him. Nearly pleading. "But I don't want to be here, either."

Sheppard was usually a man who could handle any situation, but at the moment, he was trying to remain unfazed by Fontane's inability to understand his situation. At some point he would have to. Otherwise, it would be hard for the young man to ever move on.

"But you are here, Fontane. And at some point, you need to accept that, take control of your life. You need to switch your focus to the day you will walk out of here a free man."

"A free man? Five years seems like forever."

"Less than what I'm facing. I was given thirty. I've done ten with another twenty to go. If anyone should feel depressed, it's me. Twenty years is a lot longer than five.

Like I said, you should concentrate on walking out of here one day."

"How am I supposed to do that, Sheppard?"

At least he was asking, which was something he had never done before. Another thing Fontane had never done was to call him by name. He'd always referred to him as "old man".

"First by following the rules, which will make your life a lot easier here. Then, by becoming a better human being. One who can get along with others. You need to remember that you're not the only one who doesn't want to be here. None of us do. But if we all stick together, work together and look out for each other, we'll survive this place and leave here better people."

Fontane didn't say anything. He wouldn't look at Sheppard. When he finally glanced up, Sheppard saw both pain and determination in his eyes. At that moment, a part of Sheppard believed he was finally getting through to Fontane and he couldn't help but feel good about that.

9

I got a call that you wanted to see me." Carson said, walking into the conference room.

Sheppard stood and crossed the room to stand in front of her. He was convinced she had no idea just how much he'd wanted to see her. Smiling down at her, he said, "Yes, I'm glad you came." He wrapped his arms around her. "I've missed you." As usual, she looked good and she smelled even better.

She glanced up and returned his smile. "I've missed you, too." She glanced around. "Where's Ambrose?"

"He had a few things to take care of and will return later. Much later."

"Oh."

"Oh? Sounds like you're not looking forward to being alone with me," he said teasingly, leaning down and placing kisses around her mouth and nose.

She chuckled. "Trust me, I am. I definitely don't have a problem with being alone with you, Sheppard."

"Good."

CAPTIVATED BY LOVE

He then captured her mouth, sliding his tongue between her lips and immediately feeling desire throb below his waist. Their tongues began mingling aggressively and at that moment, he couldn't get enough of her taste. The little purr that sounded from her throat goaded him to delve deeper. There was never a time when her kiss didn't captivate him.

He loved kissing her and was convinced he always would. The intensity of being with her made him forget they were in a room with no windows, a place where prison guards were patrolling the perimeters and barbed wire surrounded the facility. Any other time, focusing on such things could have a negative effect on his mentality. But thanks to Carson, all he could think about was the way he felt as his mouth clung to hers as if it was a lifeline.

His hands automatically lowered to her hips and he shifted into the curve of her body. Her closeness was like a drug, addicting him to the feel of her pressed against him. Every nerve ending within him was brutally brought to life, and as if with a mind of its own, his hand began moving, stroking her backside.

The hard tips of her nipples pressed into his chest and his erection rubbed between the symmetry of her thighs. Their tongues mated greedily, hungrily and insatiably. Their lower bodies grinded against each other relentlessly, making it harder and harder to control the pounding of his pulse. His erection rubbed against her pelvis, and the intensity of his need for her had temptation rocking through his veins.

Moans rang throughout the room. His. Hers. Theirs. Intense pleasure consumed his mind, and he was tempted to place her on the table and spread her legs. From there, he would ease her skirt up to stroke along her inner thigh. It would be so easy to slide his hand between her legs, glide that same hand beneath her panties to stroke her. Feel her wet heat. That same heat he thought about every night. Or better yet, he could unzip his pants, spread her thighs wider and enter her. God knew, a part of him was tempted.

Knowing his thoughts were traveling down a dangerous path, he broke off the kiss and gathered her into his arms, needing to hold her close. Drawing in a deep breath, his hands slowly stroked up and down her back.

"You do things to me, Carson Boyett."

"And you do things to me, Sheppard Granger."

Her words sounded so heartfelt, he was tempted to pull her back in his arms to devour her mouth again. Knowing they needed to talk, he took a step back. "I wanted to meet with you today for a reason."

She lifted a brow. "Is anything wrong?"

He saw concern in her eyes and shook his head. "No, nothing is wrong. I want to hire you as my attorney."

#

Carson blinked, certain she hadn't heard him right. "Did you say you want to hire me as your attorney?"

"Yes. I've thought about it and I don't think it would be unethical. We agreed to pursue a personal relationship weeks ago and one has nothing to do with the other."

"But what about the attorney you have now?" Although she thought the man was lousy, she would never bash a fellow attorney to his client.

He chuckled derisively. "I barely hear from him. My father has wanted me to get rid of Youngerman for years but I kept him on. Now I realize he hasn't given me the one thing you mentioned I need for myself. Hope."

"Why did you keep him on Sheppard?" That question had nagged at her since reading her research on him. Sheppard Granger was a very smart man, and he had to have known his attorney hadn't done his best. Why hadn't he fired the man before now and hired someone else?

"It's complicated Carson. There were a lot of things he could have presented during my trial that might have swayed the jury in my favor, but I wouldn't let him."

She lifted a brow. "Why?"

He drew in a deep breath. "Because it would have exposed a side of my wife I didn't want my sons to know about. Sylvia was their mother and I refused to let anyone muddy her name."

"So you let them muddy yours instead? You let your sons assume you were the bad guy? That you actually killed their mother?"

"In my heart, I don't think they believe that. They know me and wouldn't believe I could do such a thing. But

127

the newspapers were brutal. If anyone had gotten a hold of some of the things Sylvia was doing, all her affairs, they would not have hesitated to tear down her character. I couldn't do that to my sons. So I forbade Youngerman to go forward with that approach."

"And the reason you've kept him on?"

"Because he knows how I feel about things."

She nodded. "So, in other words, someone else might not be as accommodating in keeping your secrets."

"Yes."

"But what about now? Depending on what the private investigator discovers, you might have to muddy your wife's name in order to clear yours. As your attorney, I would want to reopen your case and put everything out there."

"I know. But now my sons are grown men and not teens. They're old enough to handle anything that might come out in court."

"Okay, I understand how you feel about your sons. But after reading the report on the trial, I still think the man could have fought harder for you."

"I agree. But it was only after I was convicted that I thought that way. That's why I agreed to let Dad hire a private investigator." Sheppard eased a little closer to her. "So what do you think Carson? Do you want to take me on?"

She saw the heat lining the depths of his eyes and knew the question was two-fold. "Yes, I would love taking you on, Sheppard."

A smile touched the corners of his lips. "Good. That means we'll need to meet more regularly so I can bring you up to speed."

His words came out in a deep, husky timbre that sent shivers through her body. "I can handle it."

"We'll see."

Was that a challenge he'd just issued? If so, she would show him she rarely backed down. She reached up and traced his sculpted jaw with the tip of her finger. "No, Sheppard Granger, you're the one who will see."

He wasn't given time to respond when the knock on the door signaled Ambrose's return.

10

Stop worrying. Zina is okay. She's with her daddy."

Roddran placed her cell phone down by her plate and glanced over at Carson with chagrin on her face. "I know I'm being a worrywart but this is the first time Myles has kept her by himself and--"

"He'll do fine. Have you forgotten he's the oldest of five?"

"No, but that was years ago."

"Some things you don't easily forget." Carson smiled. She had a sure fire way of shifting Roddran's attention from what was happening back at her home. "You remember a few months ago I mentioned meeting someone?" she said, stirring Roddran's memory.

"Hmm, that extremely handsome man you met at some business meeting?"

Carson chuckled, not surprised Roddran had remembered those particular details. "Yes, that's the one. Well, we've gotten serious."

Roddran's lashes flew up. "Whoa! Are you saying that you've been seeing someone and didn't tell me?"

"Something like that. You've been busy with Zina and getting ready for your move to Texas."

"No excuses, Car. I should have suspected something. You've been smiling a lot. Why haven't you brought him around?"

"There's a good reason for that."

"Which is?"

Carson took a sip of her hot tea knowing Roddran's intense gaze was watching her every move. "Because he's in jail."

Roddran blinked and then gave her one of those, *you can't be serious* looks.

"I am serious, Rod."

Roddran shook her head. "You send people to jail, not date them."

"He's different."

Roddran stared at her for a minute. "I refuse to believe you're dating a convict."

"And like I said, he's different."

"Who is he? What's he in for?"

Carson knew her response would only concern Roddran even more. "His name is Sheppard Granger and he was--"

"Sent to prison for killing his wife," Roddran finished for her. "Neither of us was living in Charlottesville at the time, but it made national news. I kept up with the trial while living in New York. He was found guilty, Car."

"I know, but he's innocent."

"He told you that?"

"Yes."

"And you believe him?"

"Yes. I believed he was innocent even before he told me he was."

Roddran obviously couldn't believe what she was hearing. "Carson, you have to be the most level-headed woman I know. Sensible. Practical. Realistic. You are not someone who would date a man in jail for murdering his wife."

"He did not murder his wife, Rod," Carson said in a firm voice, probably firmer than she'd intended. She knew her best friend loved her and wanted the best for her. But as far as she was concerned, Sheppard was the best.

"I think you need to start from the beginning," Roddran suggested.

Carson felt she needed to do so as well. So she began talking, telling Roddran how she and Sheppard had initially met and how those meetings had started every three weeks and then continued every two weeks. When she told Roddran that Sheppard had recently hired her to be his attorney, Carson had expected Roddran to break in with questions--definitely a comment or two--but she hadn't.

When Carson had finished telling her everything, Roddran drew in a deep breath and said, "Okay, let me play devil's advocate for a minute. Let's say he is innocent and this private investigator that he's hired can't help him. That's almost eight or nine years before he can be considered for parole. Would you willingly put your life on hold, tie yourself to a man who can't take you out, or spend the night with you to replace your battery-operated toy? Marry you?"

Carson met Roddran's gaze. "Yes. It might seem to you that I'd be putting my life on hold. But I would be living my life."

Roddran didn't say anything for a minute. "I read a book years ago that focused on reasons women considered getting serious about a man behind bars. For the most part, they were women who had been in prior abusive relationships. They were also women who like being in control of their lives and knowing their man is locked up gives them that control. They won't have to worry about him popping up when they might not want to be bothered. It's a kind of relationship-when-I-want-it attitude. Those were also mainly women who were emotionally damaged. That's not you, Car, even if your ex was an asshole." She shook her head. "Like I said, you are the most sensible, level-headed and realistic person I know. But then, I do know about your soft spot for underdogs. The one that came from having parents who were down-in-the-trenches community activists."

"My soft spot, as you put it, has nothing to do with anything. I care for him, Roddran. Sheppard Granger is different than any man I know. Although he's locked up for a crime he didn't commit, he still does good work." She smiled when she remembered something Sheppard once told her. "He enjoys taking lemons and making them into lemonade."

"And he's truly the man you want? No matter what?"

Carson nodded. "Yes, he is truly the man I want. No matter what."

#

Sheppard leaned back in his chair at the computer station feeling good about his father's visit. Richard had gotten a call from Imerson, who'd told him that he'd pieced together an interesting puzzle. The man had hoped to meet with the Grangers in a few weeks to bring them up to date on what he'd uncovered and felt it was the evidence needed to clear Sheppard. He wouldn't give Richard Granger any more information than that.

Sheppard couldn't help but smile. The possibility that he could be a free man soon had him elated. That meant there was a chance he could have a future with Carson. A future that wasn't hinged on stolen kisses whenever they met.

Whenever he thought about her, he couldn't help the flutters that would spread throughout his body. No woman had ever made his pulse kick up just at the sight of her, the sound of her or the smell of her. He shifted his body in the chair at the feel of an erection just from thinking about her.

Deciding to swing his thoughts elsewhere, he thought about his father.

Richard Granger had merely raised a brow when he'd told him he was getting rid of his present attorney and replacing him with Carson. Although Richard had never met Carson, he was familiar with her from all the recent news coverage on her for that huge settlement she'd gotten for her client from Perriman Department Store.

Sheppard knew his father was a little relieved he'd finally released his former attorney. The man had come highly recommended by Vidal Duncan, who was a close family friend, the company attorney for Granger Aeronautics and a man he considered a godfather.

Whenever he'd discuss reopening his case, Youngerman would usually suggest that it wouldn't be in the best interest of his sons to put them through another trial. In the past Sheppard, had conceded to Youngerman's way of thinking, but like he'd told Carson, his sons were now grown men who could handle a new trial if it came to that.

Sheppard turned his attention back to the computer screen and the information he'd researched for the past couple of weeks. It was about a form of sex, an old Hindu practice that could increase the intimacy between a man and a woman. It was emotional rather than physical. The end result was usually powerful orgasms. He'd gotten aroused just reading about it and could imagine him and

Carson trying something like this. Even now his senses were stimulated in a way that had his entire body stirred up.

At this point, anything was worth a try. It was getting harder and harder to stop kissing her, to not give in to temptation and make love to her.

He checked the clock on the wall. His meeting with Carson would be in a couple of hours. He couldn't wait to see her again.

#

Carson walked into the meeting room and couldn't help the smile that touched her lips when she saw Sheppard. Today they were holding a client-attorney meeting and she'd looked forward to it. Yesterday, she'd gotten a dozen red roses from him, with a card that read simply...*I can't wait to see you. Sheppard.*

Delvers was one of those facilities that allowed inmates to order flowers and gifts to send to their loved ones, but she'd never thought she would be the recipient of such thoughtfulness. "Good afternoon, gentlemen."

Both men returned her greeting and then after excusing himself, Ambrose left them alone. As soon as she heard the click of the door closing behind Ambrose, Sheppard moved toward her. The female in her appreciated every single thing about him. She'd never get enough of his chiseled good looks. He'd shown her pictures of his sons and they'd inherited their father's handsome features.

When he came to a stop in front of her, she inhaled his scent, an extraordinary blend of aftershave and man. And then he reached out, pulled her into his arms and claimed her mouth. The kiss was definitely what she needed right now.

Then he slid his tongue between her parted lips, tangling it with hers, kissing her more thoroughly than she'd ever been kissed. She couldn't help moaning when he deepened the kiss, zapping her senses while exploring her mouth with an expertise that sent desire plummeting through her. Everywhere his tongue touched, it sent sparks of pleasure pulsing beneath her skin, making her arch her body closer to his. She felt his erection poking hard against her.

Sheppard took the art of French kissing to a whole new level. He was definitely a pro and each time his tongue entered her mouth, she was overwhelmed by passion. Kissing had always been something she could take or leave. It had never been anything that moved her. Definitely, it was nothing that had ever made her breasts ache, her tongue tangle, her hormones rage. But all that had changed with Sheppard.

He released her mouth and she dropped her head to his chest to draw in much needed breath. The throbbing sensation coursing through her body began to slow.

"You okay?" he asked her in a throaty voice while his hand slowly stroked up and down her back. His breath was warm against her neck.

"Yes, I'm okay," she said, deciding not to tell him how his kiss had pretty much left her in a daze, leaving her drowning in sensations that still made her want to moan.

Gathering as much strength as she could, she lifted her head and met the dark penetrating eyes staring down at her. "Thanks for the flowers, Sheppard. They are beautiful."

She watched as those same lips that had practically devoured her moments ago formed into what she thought was a high-voltage sensual smile. "You are beautiful Carson. Both inside and out."

He had a way of saying things that made her feel beautiful. Made her want to be an even better individual, the beautiful person he saw her to be. Sheppard had that kind of effect on people. Knowing she couldn't stand here in his arms forever, she took a step back, immediately feeling the loss of his closeness. "Thank you." She drew in a deep breath. "So what's on the agenda today? Anything in particular we need to discuss? I got your request for a longer meeting. Is everything alright?"

He reached out and pulled her closer to him, settling her body against his. Heat curled in her stomach from his touch. His gaze held hers and the desire in his eyes made her pulse flicker. "You feel it, Carson?"

Her body seemed to blaze under his regard and she could feel her womb contract. The air seemed thick with primal need. She could sense it, feel it, nearly touch it. "Yes, I can feel it. I always do whenever we're together, Sheppard. Especially after we've kissed."

"The more I kiss you, the more I want you, Carson. And that's not good."

She decided not to remind him that it had been his decision to set the boundaries of their meetings. "I hope you're not thinking that we shouldn't ever kiss."

He looked at her with a pair of serious eyes. "No, that's not what I'm thinking, although I have to admit that had crossed my mind a few times. I've come up with an idea."

She lifted a brow. "What sort of idea?"

"Tantric sex."

11

Sheppard studied Carson's features, watching her reaction to what he'd said. He loved kissing her, but now he wanted to try something that neither one of them had done before. Not regular sex requiring a bed, entwined limbs and penetration, but one that involved a meeting of the minds, so to speak. Something more emotional than physical but just as satisfying. In some ways, even more exhilarating. Far more intimate.

"Tantric sex?" she asked.

"Yes. Ever heard of it?"

She shrugged her shoulders. "Yes, but…"

"But what?"

"Can something like that really work? Honestly? Focusing on the mental instead of the physical, meditating, barely touching, prolonging the big O. Sounds pretty much like mind-induced torture to me."

He smiled. "It's just the opposite."

She gazed at him curiously. "It sounds like you're speaking from experience."

"I don't mean to. I've never tried it. However, I've been reading a lot about it over the past few weeks."

"Why?"

"Because I see it as an alternative for us." She didn't have to ask him why he'd been looking for alternatives. Unless they did something to take the heat off, temptation would soon get the best of them.

Ambrose would deliberately allow them private time, essentially giving them the opportunity to engage in conjugal visits if they desired. And God knew, they'd been tempted more than once, when their kisses had gotten out of control. However, he didn't want to go there.

Deep down, Sheppard knew he'd fallen in love with her. He had fought it, coming up with every argument against it, but he hadn't been able to stop it from happening.

In accepting he loved her and knowing that unless Marshall Imerson's investigation turned up something that could set him free, he was faced with the reality that he was locked up for the long haul. He wouldn't be considered for parole for another eight years, which to him was nearly a lifetime. Although he wished he could be noble and give Carson up, he knew there was no way he could do so. She lit up his world in ways she would never know and had become his hope. He faced each day with more meaning and clarity because he looked forward to this. The time he would look at her, talk to her, smell her scent, share her space and taste her lips.

On the other hand, he knew Carson deserved more than a few stolen kisses. He wanted her to feel the love, the desire, the want and the need. But more than anything, he wanted her to experience the pleasure. Pleasure from him in a unique way. A profound way. An emotional way. He intended to channel all that sexual energy encasing them into gratified sensuality. And when the day came that he was released from here, he would make love to her in the traditional way. But everything they'd share now would make their first physical union that much hotter, passionate and meaningful.

They would be taking their relationship to another level. But was she open to it? In order for it to work between them, she had to be engaged, to believe in the power of their desire. She would have to be ready for them to tap into each other's sexual senses to a degree where she might feel vulnerable. She would have to let herself go and trust him fully. Could she do that?

Sheppard leaned his hip against the table and held her gaze intently. He would be honest with her, explain what he wanted to do, but first, he wanted to share his feelings so she would understand why he wanted to try such a thing.

He tightened his hold on her hand while feeling the soothing undercurrent of desire pass between them. In their touch alone was everything he'd need to make his case. It was time they channeled all that energy into pleasure.

"I've fallen in love with you, Carson. I know it might sound unbelievable to you considering everything, especially our circumstances. But I have, which is why I need a deeper connection to you. Of course, if you don't feel the same, I will understand if you want no part in what I'm suggesting."

#

Happiness curled in Carson's stomach and a smile spread across her lips. She couldn't believe Sheppard had just admitted to loving her and wanted to quickly arrest his doubts. "I love you too, Sheppard."

She saw the look of surprise in his eyes. "You do?"

"Yes. I think I fell in love with you the day we first met."

A huge smile touched his lips. "Funny, you should say that because if I was asked, I would say walking into Warden Smallwood's office and seeing you would be the defining moment for me as well. I think I fell in love with you the moment I looked into your eyes."

"Oh, Sheppard."

Tightening his arms around her waist, he drew her to him. She rested her head on his chest, fighting to breathe as happiness grabbed her by the throat. This man loved her. She loved him. Confessing their love was the first step and she was willing to take many more steps with him. Since Pence, she'd avoided men. But now, she believed Sheppard had been brought into her life for a reason. Just like she believed one day, he would walk out of here a free man, exonerated of all charges. Her goal as the woman he loved and the woman who loved him was to keep that hope alive. No matter what.

"So the question I have for you, Carson, is…are you absolutely sure you want to hang in with me for the long-haul, not knowing how long that will be?"

She wrapped her arms around his neck and met his gaze. "Let's shoot on forever. I will be yours forever, Sheppard, through thick and thin. In prison or out. I won't be just your prison babe."

He smiled. "You could never be just a prison babe. You and I are too old for that. I want to shoot for forever as well. The day I am released from this place, I will walk out with my head held high knowing the woman I love will be waiting for me. And on that day, or as soon as it can be arranged, I want to make you mine legally."

She blinked, not sure what he was saying.

Obviously noticing her confusion, he added, "I mean that more than anything, Carson Boyett, I want you to become Mrs. Sheppard Granger one day." He paused a minute. "But for now, there have to be conditions."

Happiness nearly overwhelmed her. "More conditions, Sheppard?"

"Yes."

"And what are these conditions?"

He held her gaze for a long moment. "I will tell my father about us, but I'm not ready to share any details of our relationship with anyone else yet, including my sons.

My life has pretty much been an open book, but I'd like to keep you as the one part that remains private."

He paused. "I want to protect you from the ridicule of becoming involved with a convicted killer."

She shook her head. "I don't care about that, Sheppard."

"But I do care. I can just imagine the damage it could cause your business, one you've built over the years because of your stellar reputation. I refuse to have anyone start questioning your judgement because of your involvement with me."

Carson didn't care about any of that, but seeing the firm set of his jaw, she knew Sheppard would not be swayed. This would be one of those topics they would have to discuss again later, but for now she would agree.

"Okay, Sheppard. But I have a condition of my own."

He lifted a brow. "What condition is that?" She could tell by his tone he was somewhat leery about what she would say.

"I know you won't consider us making out in here, but if you're serious about this tantric sex thing, then I want to experience it with you every chance we get."

She heard him release his breath. "We will, when reasonably possible. But first we need to determine if it's something you want to indulge in. I thought we would get things started today. Are you ready for it?"

She couldn't hide the excitement she knew he saw in her eyes. "Yes, Sheppard, I'm definitely all in."

12

Sheppard couldn't stop the smile that curved his lips. He was tempted to lean over and kiss Carson again but their class in TS 101 needed to begin. He felt certain this was something they both would enjoy. "Come on, let's get started," he said, taking her hand and leading her over to a chair.

Since this was a client/attorney meeting, they would not be disturbed. The situation was just about perfect.

"Now what Sheppard?"

They sat beside each other, holding hands. Twisting around in the chair he stared at her, thinking that there were so many things about Carson that touched him, made him appreciate being a male. The man who loved her. At night, he would lie in bed and imagine being somewhere else-- namely in some other bed with her lying beside him. He'd fantasize about all the things he would do to her. However, despite the erotic thoughts that would filter through his mind while lying there and craving her physically, there was an inner part of him that yearned for a mental connection to her as well.

That was the one thing he and Sylvia had never shared. An emotional bond. They'd married young, with sex foremost on their minds. She'd been as insatiable in bed as he'd been. As a young man, he'd had an unquenchable sexual appetite. Now he was old enough to know sex alone could not hold a relationship together. There had to be more.

"Now we sit here and stare into each other eyes for a while, Carson," he said softly.

"Why? Am I supposed to read something in yours?"

He heard the curiosity in her voice. "In a way. But the main reason is to expand the intimacy between us. Deepen it. Develop a close connection between us that's not just sexual. We'll close our eyes for a while first. Then when you think you feel a mental bond forming, open them. Just gaze deeply into my eyes to continue the relationship building."

Carson nodded. "Okay."

She closed her eyes and he closed his. He wasn't sure what she was thinking about, but he focused his mind on the feeling of having her hand in his. He brushed a thumb back and forth over her palm, loving the feel of her soft skin. Remembering how that same thumb had once gently touched her face and how his fingertips had slid over her cheeks and lips. His body tingled with awareness.

Breathing slowly, he inhaled her scent and leaned closer to get more of it. He could actually feel the way the air around them seemed to overflow with sexual energy.

Something stirred to life in his mid-section as he continued to smell her, accept her feminine nearness and recognized the pull of desire stimulating his gut.

Sheppard slowly opened his eyes to look at Carson and saw that her eyes were still closed. He wasn't sure what thoughts consumed her mind but whatever they were, soft sighs were floating from her lips. He doubted she was aware she was making them. The subtle sounds stirred the air and stroked the space separating them. A feeling of peace and harmony flowed through him, overflowing right into his soul. It was then he realized just how close their faces were and decided to take advantage of the proximity to study her features while undisguised love warmed his heart.

His gaze was drawn to her lips--lips that held him mesmerized whenever he looked at her for too long. Lips he enjoyed kissing. Just the thought sent sparks of energy charging in the room. But it wasn't the typical sexual energy. What he was beginning to feel was unhurried euphoria, a state of contentment that filled his lungs with deep, satisfying breaths.

Dark lashes were lowered over her closed eyes and seeing such a serene look on her face set off a ripple of burning desire through him. He was counting on another kind of intimacy for him and Carson, one that lasted longer, and was far deeper than anything either of them could imagine. He was feeling it already.

He'd been about to shift his gaze when she slid her eyes open and their gazes connected.

#

The task had been for them to silently build an inner connection and it hadn't taken long for her to feel it. Ridding her mind of clients and the cases that came with them hadn't been easy. But once she filled her thoughts with Sheppard, she hadn't wanted to focus on anything else.

She had reflected on his charm, his goodness, and how, even after having his freedom taken away, he'd somehow maintained a stateliness, a charismatic air, an appealing persona. He was such a distinguished individual and being locked up hadn't taken that away from him. She was filled with happiness that such a man could love her.

Concentrating on him also meant focusing on the time they'd spent together getting to know each other. She imagined she could feel his warm breath close to her face. And then when she'd been consumed with thoughts of him, she had opened her eyes to find him there, staring at her.

At that moment, she'd been wholly conscious of him and everything about him. Unable to break eye contact, she'd felt so much energy flowing from him that the magnitude made her limbs tremble and her skin tingle. The sexy eyes staring at her were so mesmerizing, she shivered with desire. Wild swirls of need encompassed her with burning intensity. How could she feel this way from just staring into his eyes?

Carson knew she was seeing Sheppard as the man he truly was. Uncovered and uncensored. The skin on her hand burned where he held it. Every fiber in her body felt alive and she was able to sense something else about him. It was love. She could actually feel his love for her. Total joy filled her soul, elation touched her heart and a degree of exultation surrounded her.

She knew they had a rocky road ahead. There was no way they couldn't. There might come a time when he would try pushing her away again, but she would always stand her ground with him. Making Sheppard a part of her life had been what she wanted. He'd told her she deserved more, but she knew that they deserved each other. Her mind overflowed with the love they shared. They were truly connected.

She watched as his lips slowly vibrated whenever he breathed in through his nose and out from his mouth. And the color of his pupils seemed to be a dark navy rather than a midnight black.

A sensual mist surrounded them. A flutter began low in her stomach and her arms felt as if they were being caressed, when all he did was hold her hand in his. No words were spoken between them and she knew none were needed. Not when a throbbing began escalating slowly and meticulously between her legs. And as he continued to hold her in a daze-like state, she felt a flow of heat convulse her insides. A degree of pleasure filled her and she wished she could lean into him. Draw on his strength while her heart swelled with love. So much love.

He was looking at her with an intensity that went beyond just physical need. She saw desire and a ferocious longing within the dark depths of his eyes, but she also saw something else, something that nearly made her gasp out loud. It was a yearning to be a part of her--heart, soul, body and mind. She was slowly being bombarded with sensation after sensation. What she felt warmed her heart and filled her with a sense of deep satisfaction. The realization that she was loved and desired so forcefully was slowly plunging her body into a state of mind-blowing ecstasy.

Her breasts tingled, her skin began to feel hot and a deep throbbing grew between her legs…all from the way he was looking at her. The entire room seemed to radiate their heat. The air they breathed fanned the flames, engulfing their bodies with a kind of passion she doubted even touching could evoke.

She noticed he wasn't immune to what was taking place. She didn't have to reach out to touch the crotch of his pants to see that he was aroused. It was obvious in everything about him. The way drops of moisture appeared on his forehead. How his skin appeared strained and pulled tight over his cheekbones. The way his jaw was thrusting forward. How his firm mouth seemed set, on the edge of control.

Following his lead, she began breathing deeply through her nose and exhaling through slightly parted lips. Doing so seemed to heighten the shared sensuality, boosting it to an even higher level. The sensations flowing through her began taking over of their own volition. Her spine arched and her thighs opened, releasing all the volatile heat between her legs. Heat she wasn't capable of controlling. Something was stimulating her down there, at the very core of her center.

Spikes of spasms began traveling from her thighs and up her abdomen to her breasts. Their movement was slow and deliberate, inflaming every inch of skin. She became even more aware of the drugging scent of him. The sound of his breathing. The way his hand tightened on hers.

Then it happened. Spontaneously.

She climaxed hard, sitting right there in a chair staring eye to eye with him. When they whispered each other's names, she knew what had taken place. It wasn't the same kind of orgasm that came when lovemaking was just physical. It was something entirely different, something more powerful. It had the ability to connect the physical with the emotional in a way that encompassed all five senses. It had started out subtle then slowly escalated to something truly formidable.

She continued to study Sheppard and saw that, like hers, his body was gearing up for yet another orgasm. How was that possible? Yet the shudders that were beginning to invade her body were a tell-tale sign. His nostrils were flaring from the depth of his breathing and the heavy sound of their laborious panting galvanized the room, stirring sensual energy.

How long could a person endure such sexual empowerment? She wasn't sure but was more than eager to find out. And from the look in Sheppard's eyes, so was he.

#

Sheppard thought there was nothing like the scent of an aroused woman. The area below his below his waist seemed ready to explode again. He'd never appreciated it until now and wondered how he'd successfully managed to put such a thing way to the back of his mind. The last thing a man who was destined to be locked up for a long time should have on his mind was his need for a woman. He'd been well aware that a number of the men at Glenworth had engaged with flings with some of the female prison guards or managed quickies with wives, girlfriends or significant others. But he had accepted his fate. His sex life had ended long before Sylvia had died. In his mind, he couldn't miss something he rarely got anyway.

What he shared with Carson was special. He'd treasured each and every kiss. But what he'd just shared with her had been something totally unexpected. Even now, his body was still wired up, his senses heightened to a degree he hadn't thought possible.

If they could share something like this by using just the energy in the room, he didn't want to think how things would be if they combined traditional lovemaking with tantric sex. He couldn't imagine any other woman as the giver and recipient of something so over the top mind-blowing.

Unless he finally brought this session to an end, they could continue stimulating their senses this way for hours. That was a luxury they didn't have but they could look forward to the next time.

Sheppard leaned closer to Carson's mouth and captured it in his, showing her everything he felt for her in his kiss. Slowly and seductively, he savored her taste, yearning for the next time. Knowing there would be a next time sent his spirits soaring. He released her mouth and stared into her eyes before they moved to rake boldly over her. At that moment, everything felt right in his world.

Raising their joined hands to his lips, he kissed them, using his tongue to lick her knuckles. He heard her sharp intake of breath. "You okay, Carson?" he asked as his steady gaze bore into her, knowing he'd just shared a kind of intimacy with her that he hadn't with any other woman.

"Only you can ask me something like that, Sheppard," she said as a smile touched her lips. "You are like a magnet."

"So are you," he countered, kissing their joined hands again.

"What we just shared was special. So very special," she whispered. "I didn't know that such a thing was possible."

He hadn't truly known either until he'd done the research. Now he was glad he had.

"I'm looking forward to our next meeting, Sheppard," she said quietly.

A smile touched his lips. "So am I, baby. So am I."

Sheppard then leaned in and took her mouth in his again, gently at first and then with a hunger he felt all the way to the groin. He would never tire of kissing her, touching her, sharing intimacies with her. He loved her and believed one day he would be set free and then he could give her his name and the kind of life she deserved.

13

Sheppard inhaled a shocked breath as he gazed at his father. "Marshall Imerson is dead? But how? When?" Ambrose had left them alone so they could talk privately. His heart went out to Imerson's wife and son, grieving for their loss.

Richard Granger dragged in a deep breath as well. "An auto accident. I heard about it on the news this morning. They're claiming Marshall was killed while driving under the influence."

Sheppard studied his father. "DWI? But I thought Imerson didn't drink."

"He didn't."

Sheppard knew there was more. "What is it, Dad? Tell me."

Richard rubbed a hand down his face. "On the way here, someone leaked a rumor to the media that there were financial problems within his company and that he was involved in something illegal. I don't believe any of that either. All I know is that he'd discovered something big with Sylvia's murder which could have exonerated you of all charges. I have no idea what he'd found out and I have a feeling he died because of it."

Sheppard didn't say anything for a long moment, but he had that same sinking feeling. He knew he hadn't killed his wife. And for years, he'd wondered who had. Sylvia Granger's killer was still out there and evidently was determined not to be exposed. Now, more than ever, he believed Sylvia's death had nothing to do with her numerous affairs. But if not her affairs, then what? If his suspicions were true, then trying to expose her killer might place his sons and father in danger. Had Imerson's death been a warning?

"You okay, Sheppard?"

It would be so easy to lie and say that he was, but he couldn't. Although he'd told Carson not to get her hopes up that Imerson might find something to make him a free man, he had done the unthinkable and gotten his own hopes up. Each time he saw Carson, he'd wanted to believe that his time behind bars would soon come to an end. Imerson had been excited about whatever he'd uncovered and had refused to share it with anyone. Unfortunately, that meant whatever he'd dug up had gone to the grave with him.

He saw the worried look on his father's face. "Yes, Dad. I'm fine. But I prefer if we keep our suspicions about Imerson's death to ourselves and not share them with anyone. Not Jace, Caden or Dalton. Hannah or anyone."

Richard nodded. "Will you tell Carson Boyett what we suspect?"

Sheppard slumped his shoulders. "No. At least not now. If I were to tell her, she might want to hire that PI she works with to take over Imerson's investigation and I can't let that happen." He couldn't help but remember how her life had been placed in danger when she'd re-opened Roland Summer's case. If anything were to happen to her because of him… He drew in a deep breath. "And Dad?"

"Yes?"

"Because we have no idea who we're dealing with, I suggest you not hire another PI to clear me."

"Are you giving up Sheppard? Don't you want to be free?" Richard Granger asked with concern.

"Of course I do. But I refuse to risk anyone else's life. If what you and I suspect is true, then whoever killed Sylvia will stop at nothing to make sure they aren't exposed. We need to just let it go for now…until I can come up with another strategy, another plan." *One that won't put the people I love at risk.* "Promise me you'll do that."

Silence filled the room and then Richard Granger clapped his hand on his son's shoulder. "All right. I promise to do as you ask, Sheppard. For now."

#

Later that night, Sheppard paced the confines of his jail cell with thoughts of Marshall Imerson weighing heavily on his mind. The more he thought about it, the more he was glad he and his father had agreed to keep their suspicions to themselves. It would serve no purpose to get others involved. Especially when he had no idea who he was dealing with. But he wouldn't give up. He would continue to do research. His father had asked him more than once over the years if he had any idea who might have wanted to kill Sylvia, but he'd admitted honestly that he was clueless. He'd known Sylvia's secrets even when she thought he hadn't. Evidently, he hadn't known all of them.

His thoughts shifted to Carson. Thinking of her kept him motivated and he refused to give up the belief that one day the two of them would be together beyond the walls of Delvers. He woke up every morning in a state of happiness because he had her in his life. She was his rock and his strength. And he couldn't lose that. He couldn't lose her. She, his sons, his father and Hannah were the people who meant the most to him.

Carson was now his in all the ways that mattered and he loved her with every part of his being. He believed that one day things would be different for them. That he would be a free man. And when that day came, he would bask in what he knew was a forever kind of love with her. That was his hope. His dream. What kept him going, day after day.

No matter what, he had to keep believing. And he would.

PART TWO
THE PRESENT

The future depends on what we do in the present. –
Mahatma Gandhi

14

Carson Boyett Granger slowly opened her eyes as she curled into the heat of her husband's body. Early morning rays from the sun dipped across the bedroom denoting a brand new day. Waking up with her body plastered to Sheppard's had been the norm for the past three-hundred and sixty-five days.

After making love to start off their day, they would stand together with their arms wrapped around each other to stare out the window to watch the sun rise over the mountains.

An overwhelming feeling of love settled around her heart as she glanced over at him while he still slept. She thought the same thing now that she had when they'd first met six years ago. Sheppard Granger was an extremely handsome man. He had a certain sexiness that could make her hot all over just from looking at him. Even now, her heart was pounding wildly against her ribs and she felt a tingling sensation between her legs.

Happiness surged inside of her. Yesterday they'd celebrated their first wedding anniversary and although they'd agreed not to exchange gifts, he had surprised her with one anyway. A beautiful diamond necklace. It had almost brought tears to her eyes when she'd seen it. She had married such a loving and giving man. He gave so much of himself to others and asked for nothing in return. The mere fact that he'd fallen in love with her and had wanted her as his mate for life was still overwhelming at times.

Since returning to Sutton Hills, Sheppard seemed more relaxed, laid-back and untroubled. Although she knew that he was glad to finally be free after serving fifteen years for a crime he didn't commit, she also knew that he often thought about the young men he'd left behind. Men who'd considered Sheppard as a father figure, a leader, a man they admired. That's why she wasn't surprised by what he'd told her last night about handing over the running of Granger Aeronautics to his oldest son, Jace, while Sheppard pursued other things.

During the first year of its existence, the Sheppard Granger Foundation for Troubled Teens had become a beacon of hope for so many. But Carson knew her husband wanted to do even more.

Glancing at the clock on the nightstand, she saw it was after seven already. Typically she would be up and dressed by now, but she had no regrets in oversleeping this morning. Not when she'd spent the better part of last night making love with her husband.

Shudders passed through her when she recalled the kisses he'd trailed down her body, the way he'd touched every inch of her skin and the words he'd whispered, escalating her desire and skyrocketing her passion.

As far as she was concerned, no one could make love better than Sheppard Granger. His brand of foreplay, the mix of tantric sex to stimulate her imagination, and traditional physical sex, where he would spread her legs and enter her body, made her breath catch between a sigh and a throaty moan.

"You said something, baby?"

The deep, husky sound of her husband's voice sent sensuous chills through her. Total awareness of him filled her every cell. She tilted her head and looked up into his face, immediately feeling a deep stirring in her mid-section. The neatly trimmed salt and pepper beard slashed across the rugged angles of his sculpted jaw, emanated sexy maturity meshed with raw male sensuality.

Her gaze slid to his lips and she struggled with the impulse to lean up and take them with hers. Instead she stared at them, remembering how he'd used them on her during the night. All over her body.

"Carson?"

He was awake and she loved how he would say her name, dragging the last syllable out with a sexy drawl. "No, I didn't say anything. I was just thinking. Remembering last night and how we celebrated our first wedding anniversary."

"Umm," he said, tightening his arms around her. "Did it meet with your approval?"

A smile touched her lips. "Immensely, but then, so has every day since marrying you."

"You deserve everything you get, sweetheart. I don't know of any other woman who would have stuck by my side for five solid years. I will love you forever for doing so."

As far as she was concerned, it had been the best five years of her life. Sheppard had been her beacon of hope. And true to his word, it hadn't been a full twenty-four hours after being released from Delvers when he'd married her.

"And I will forever love you, too, Sheppard." In her heart, she meant it.

"How do you feel today?" he asked her.

Over the past few weeks, she'd battled a queasy stomach, but had felt fine for the past couple of days. "Okay. It's probably nothing more than a stomach virus. But I do need to call the doctor anyway to schedule my annual physical and see about getting my flu shot."

"Good idea. I need to get a flu shot as well. The last thing I want is for either of us to be sick...especially when there are so many bedroom activities we enjoy. Like this."

He lowered his head and slid his tongue inside her mouth. She couldn't help the purr that settled deep in her throat. Instantly, passion consumed her.

His tongue mingled with hers and Carson felt tremors invade her body. When he deepened the kiss, full sexual charges zapped her senses. Their limbs were entwined and she could feel the hardness of his erection press into her. Of their own accord, her legs eased opened and he shifted their positions to place her beneath him. It always amazed her just how perfectly he fit between her legs, and how his intimate touches seemed to be made only for her.

He stared down at her and immediately she felt emotions flowing out of him and pouring straight into her. Thanks to tantric sex, it was something that always happened whenever their gazes locked for any period of time. As if consumed by something surging within him, he whispered her name while easing inside of her.

A jolt of sexual delight crammed her and she could feel the hot throbbing of his erection invade her body in a way that made her moan. Feminine inner muscles clenched him and electrified her senses. Spikes of pounding pleasure ricocheted all through her. She felt wired with need. Tossed over the edge. Shaken to the core and rocked in one miraculous sensation after another.

When he began to thrust hard in a steady rhythm that had blood rushing through her veins, she couldn't stop the whispered purr of sexual bliss sounding deep in her throat. Managing to pull her mouth away from him, she cried out as shudders of orgasmic pleasure ripped through her.

"I love it whenever I feel you come," Sheppard murmured against his wife's lips.

The tantric sex they'd shared for nearly five years had been off the charts, building an emotional connection between them that might not have existed otherwise. But tantric, combined with this, the deep penetration of his body into hers, was both an emotional and physical experience that took them on a level that did more than stimulate their senses. It elevated both the love and desire that encompassed them.

Instead of shifting his body off her, Sheppard felt another orgasm rolling in and kept thrusting inside of her, inciting more erotic energy. A slow ripple effect spread through different parts of his body, and he was determined that she feel them as well.

"Sheppard..."

His name was an intense whisper of longing and need. He leaned down and captured her mouth with a hunger and greed he wanted her to feel. He loved his wife's taste and he enjoyed making love to her in ways he'd only dreamed about while confined. Now he was free to indulge whenever and for however long he wanted. There were times when he couldn't get enough of her and now was one of those times.

The chemistry between them was just as explosive as it had always been. His goal in life was to love her forever. Protect her and cherish her. She was more than the woman who wore his name. Carson was the woman who controlled his heart and captivated his love. And because of her, he felt like a man on top of the world.

#

"We're getting too old for this."

Carson smiled as she eased her body off Sheppard's. "Speak for yourself, old man. Your young wife isn't complaining."

She glanced over at the clock on the nightstand. "We missed breakfast."

"I didn't."

His words caused arousal to flow through her body when she recalled having his head between her legs and how he'd practically made a meal of her. Each time his tongue had licked her clit she had moaned his name, begged him to stop and in the same breath, begged him to continue.

Carson released a deep breath while staring up at the ceiling. She was determined to chill a while, to allow the feverish pitch that he'd stroked her body into since she woke up hours ago, to gradually subside. There wasn't a part of her body he hadn't touched or tasted and she doubted she could handle any more right now. "You're right, you didn't. And I recall you being quite greedy."

He chuckled and the husky sound was a turn-on. Everything about Sheppard turned her on. "I plan to keep you on your back every chance I get," he said, rubbing his nose against her neck while he intermittently stroked her naked thigh.

"Hey, aren't you the one who just claimed we were too old for this?" she asked grinning. "Not that I agree with that assessment."

"I gave you fair warning that we'd make up for lost time once I left Delvers. And although I really do think we're too old for all this, I can't see us stopping any time soon."

She couldn't see that either. During the five years of his confinement, they'd managed to share a very unique kind of relationship. One based on love and not lust, where their intimate goal hadn't been focused on orgasms but primarily on stimulating their senses in a way that was even more satisfying.

They had definitely taken the art of tantric sex to a whole other level. Indulging in both kinds of eroticism was a sexual ecstasy unlike any other. They were enjoying the best of both worlds.

"What are your plans today?"

She glanced over at him. "I'm meeting Roland for lunch. Today is his and Becca's wedding anniversary. Had she lived, they would be celebrating twenty years together."

He nodded and leaned down and placed a kiss on her lips. "I can imagine how he must be feeling today. Although our relationship was at an all-time low when Sylvia died, I still think about her on birthdays and anniversaries. I try to remember the good times and how things were in the beginning. Especially during the birth of our sons. I truly believed those were our happiest times."

Carson recalled Becca telling her that she and Roland wanted to start a family once he was released from prison. She could never forget the longing in Becca's voice whenever she talked about it. She knew that had been Roland's one regret, not giving Becca the child she wanted. Whenever Becca would bring it up, Roland would convince her that it would be best to wait for a better time. Unfortunately, that *better* time never came for them.

Carson then considered her own situation. Like Becca, motherhood had always been something she'd wanted. So she'd been excited about her pregnancy, although it hadn't been planned. Pence on the other hand, had been furious. He'd even stopped speaking to her for a full month, claiming she'd deliberately gotten pregnant.

She had been happy about her pregnancy. Overjoyed. And had looked forward to the day she would bring her baby home from the hospital. She had selected a lot of names, but had decided not to find out the sex of the child until it was born. Unfortunately, she'd miscarried at fourteen weeks.

Her in-laws had taken the loss just as hard as she had, since it would have been their first grandchild. Pence, however, hadn't cared who knew he was glad she'd lost the baby. He hadn't wanted it anyway. That's when she'd left him, refusing to remain married to a man who couldn't mourn the loss of a child he'd help to create.

She shifted her thoughts from Pence to Sheppard and how different the two men were. Sheppard was the kind of husband any woman would dream of having. Her love for him grew every day. And she was building a close relationship with his sons and their wives. She couldn't help feeling thankful for the family he was sharing with her.

All three of his sons were tall, dark and extremely handsome men like their father. Jace was the oldest and married to Shana. They had a newborn son, Rylan. Shana owned a crisis management firm and the two met when Jace hired her to help bring Granger Aeronautics out of the red.

Caden was the middle son and a Grammy award winning musician. He was known worldwide as the man with the saxophone. He was married to his childhood sweetheart Shiloh, who owned a wine boutique in historical downtown. The two of them lived in the apartment above the shop.

Dalton was the youngest son and had married Jules Bradford less than a year ago on New Year's Day. Jules was a private investigator and was also Shana's sister.

"And considering everything, I'm glad Roland has you for a friend," Sheppard interrupted her thoughts to say.

"Thanks."

That was one of the reasons she loved Sheppard so much. Because he loved and trusted her, he accepted her close relationship with Roland. And after meeting Roland and getting to know him, she knew Sheppard considered Roland a good friend as well.

"Are you still going into the office today?" she asked.

"Yes and I plan to remain all day."

She cuddled closer into his arms. "When will you tell them that you prefer heading the foundation instead of returning to the company full time?"

"Not sure. There's no rush since I won't be making a final decision on anything until after the holidays."

"Good idea. In the end, you should do what makes you happy, Sheppard, even if it means turning the running of Granger Aeronautics over to your sons. I believe they will understand."

A part of him believed that as well. "I'll be meeting with Striker, Quasar and Stonewall later today, after I leave the office. I invited them to join me at Canary's for drinks. Thought I'd talk to them, find out how they're doing. Roland has been keeping them busy."

"That's a good thing, isn't it?"

"Yes, it definitely is. You want to meet up later? What about dinner at Fleurie's?"

"Dinner at Fleurie's sounds nice. After lunch with Roland, I'm headed into the office. Text me later with a time that works for you."

He leaned down and brushed a kiss on her lips again. "Thanks for always believing in me."

She reached up and stroked his bearded jaw. "I'll always believe in you, Sheppard." Leaning up she captured his mouth in a kiss.

15

Sheppard drew in a deep breath as he looked around his office at Granger Aeronautics. It was hard to believe sometimes that he was really a free man and Sylvia's killers had been brought to justice. Because Richard Granger believed that one day his son would be freed from jail, he'd mandated that everything remain intact. The first time Sheppard entered his office after his release, it was as if he'd walked back in time. The same office furniture, drapes and carpet filled the room. The desktop computer was also the same one he'd once used, although it was almost useless now.

Walking over to the window, he looked out and recalled the many times he'd stood in this very spot. It had been years but the view of the Blue Ridge Mountains was still as beautiful as he remembered. He did notice a number of steel skyscrapers that hadn't been there before and the number of restaurants jamming the downtown corridors was daunting. It was good to see how much the city had grown and spread.

He'd once been appointed by the mayor to sit on a board that had supported that very thing, new construction and a way to utilize old buildings. Instead of tearing them down, he had recommended converting them into highly attractive commercial real estate. Several members of the board had called his ideas ludicrous. He was glad some other ludicrous person whose ideas had practically mirrored his had finally gotten through to the old guard--those city leaders who hadn't been ready to embrace growth and prosperity. Charlottesville had grown and the population had grown with it. He was proud of the city where he'd been born.

He continued looking out the window for a few more minutes before walking over to his desk to trace a finger across the smooth surface. This had been his first desk at Grangers Aeronautics. A gift from his parents. In fact, most of the furniture in here had been from them. Sylvia had decorated the sitting area of his office. But as far as he knew, she hadn't known about the secret compartment in the sofa. He'd discovered it by accident one night while working late, when he'd decided to spend the night at the office instead of going home. It had been in that secret compartment that he'd hidden the photographs he'd received in the mail. Proof that his wife was having an affair.

Sheppard pushed the memory to the back of his mind. That had been years ago and there was no reason to think about it now. So many changes had occurred in his life since then. Positive changes and the main one was Carson. He couldn't help but smile whenever he thought about his wife. She was the joy of his life. People always said good things came to those who wait. He hadn't realized he'd been waiting until the moment Carson walked into his life. And she'd definitely been worth waiting for.

He glanced around upon hearing the knock on his door. "Come in."

The door opened and his three sons came in. Pride filled Sheppard's heart whenever he remembered how young they'd been when he'd gone to jail. Now they were adults. Married adults. Jace was even a father.

All three wore huge smiles. "Dad, welcome back. How does it feel?" Jace asked, standing tall with his hands shoved into his pockets.

Before he could answer, Dalton piped in. "That's a stupid question, Jace. Of course he's going to say it feels great when this is probably the last place he wants to be."

Caden frowned. "And how you figure that?"

Dalton rolled his eyes. "Why would he want to be here, when he could be back at Sutton Hills with Carson? Come on guys. Think about it. If either of us was given the chance to choose between spending a day at the office or a day at home with our wives, which would you do?"

"Our wives, as well as Carson, have jobs, Dalton. Or have you forgotten?" Jace asked, shaking his head. "That means they wouldn't be home anyway. The only reason Shana is working from home is because of Rylan."

"Yes, but if they were home, I would prefer being there any day of the week," Dalton said smiling broadly.

"I believe you," Caden said. "Jules is not at home but from what I hear, you're at her office behind closed doors every day during lunch."

Dalton chuckled. "Don't hate, Caden. Maybe you need to show up and sweep Wine Lady off her feet during lunch every once in a while."

Sheppard couldn't help but grin at the camaraderie between his sons. They got along...most of the time. But leave it to Dalton to ruffle feathers every chance he got. But then, he wouldn't be Dalton if he didn't. At least Jace and Caden didn't seem bothered by the nicknames Dalton had given their wives. He referred to Shana as Wonder Woman. Shiloh was Wine-lady. And he'd given his own wife, Jules, the nickname of Whirlwind.

"I'm happy to be here," Sheppard said, breaking up the argument. "It brings back a lot of memories. However, I will admit that it's hard being here without Dad." Richard Granger had died last year of a heart attack.

He sighed. "Dad would knock on that connecting door and I could tell from his knock if it was a visit to talk about the football game or if the visit centered mainly on business."

"A part of me regrets not having worked here while he was alive," Jace said pensively.

Caden nodded. "A part of me feels the same way."

Dalton snorted. "Hell, I don't. The old man would have worked me to death. He would have squashed any affairs I might have cultivated. He would have--"

"Kept you in line," Jace supplied.

"He would have tried," Dalton quipped.

There was a knock on the door. "Come in," Sheppard said.

A middle-aged woman who worked as an executive assistant walked in carrying a huge potted plant. "This arrived for you, Mr. Granger."

"Thanks," Sheppard said, taking the plant from the woman and sitting it on his desk. Once she left, he pulled off the card which read... *Enjoy your day at work. Love you, Carson.*

He smiled and glanced over at his sons. "It's from Carson."

"That was nice of Wedded Bliss."

Sheppard lifted a brow. "Wedded Bliss?"

"Yes, that's my nickname for Carson. If you ask me, she hasn't stopped smiling since the wedding."

Wedded Bliss. Sheppard couldn't hold back his chuckle. The name fit. And he intended to keep Carson happy. Blissfully wedded.

"So, what's on the agenda for today?" he decided to ask in an attempt to switch the topic of conversation to business before Dalton got too carried away and really ticked his brothers off.

"I think we need to update your office for starters," Dalton said, glancing around. "Bring you into the twenty-first century. You can keep the furniture if you like due to its sentimental value but that computer has to go. It's not even hooked up to the company's main server."

Sheppard nodded in agreement. "I'd like to keep the furniture but you can replace everything else."

"Good."

"As far as meetings," Jace interjected. "We're due for one in an hour. I think it's time we discussed the changing of the guard, don't you?"

Sheppard shook his head. "No. I think you're handling things just fine, Jace. There's no rush for me. Is there a reason you want me to take over?"

Jace shook his head. "No, I just assumed you'd want to reclaim your position here."

Sheppard knew now would be a good time to let his sons know exactly how he felt, but he decided the best approach would be to show them how well they could do without his interference. "I'm in no hurry. I need to get re-acclimated. Fifteen years is a long time."

"But you stayed sharp," Caden said. "Look how easily you've aced those licensing exams."

Sheppard shrugged. "I read a lot in prison. Stayed abreast of current events and embraced the computer age. It was a matter of developing good study habits." He paused a minute. "The three of you have done an outstanding job without me or Dad to help you. I am proud of you. Now you have a legacy to pass on to Rylan, Jace. And to any kids you might have in the future, Caden and Dalton."

"Hey, don't rush anything. Jules and I are having too much fun to even think about being parents. Hell, keeping up with Jules is enough. I can't imagine keeping up with her and a baby, too." Dalton said.

When Caden didn't say anything, everyone looked in his direction. A smile touched his lips. "Now is just as good a time as any to announce that Shiloh and I are expecting."

"Damn," Dalton said, as if pained. "Doesn't anyone believe in birth control anymore?"

"We were trying to have a baby, Dalton. It *wasn't* an accident." Caden said, narrowing his eyes at his brother. "Everybody isn't anti-child."

Dalton rolled his eyes. "Hey, I'm not anti-child. I love spending time with Rylan but when I'm through, I get to leave him at Jace's house. You don't see me taking him home, do you? I happen to like my wife's undivided attention. I'm not ready to compete."

Sheppard heard what his youngest son was saying, but he would bet any amount of money that Dalton's words were more bluster than anything. If Jules was to get pregnant, he'd be damn happy about it. Sheppard knew his son would be nothing like the man Carson had been married to.

"You are so selfish," Jace said to Dalton, shaking his head. "It's not all about you."

"And what's wrong with me thinking that it is?" Dalton retorted.

Deciding to step in before a full argument ensued, Sheppard walked over to Caden and gave him a bear hug. "Congratulations, Caden. I'm very happy for you and Shiloh." He was well aware Caden and Shiloh had lost a baby a few years ago and had been eager to have another. "I'll look forward to another grandchild."

"Thanks, Dad." Caden said smiling. "Shiloh and I are extremely happy about it."

"Will Shiloh tell her mother? Sheppard asked. Shiloh and her mother shared a strained relationship. Sandra Timmons had kept secrets from her daughter. They were secrets Shiloh was still trying to forgive her mother for. Secrets that had caused a number of people a lot of pain.

"Yes. Ms. Timmons is out of town for the holidays. We intend to tell her when she returns after New Year's."

"Good. This will be Sandra's first grandchild and a baby might repair Sandra and Shiloh's relationship. Mend the hurt."

"Possibly."

Sheppard could tell by his son's response that he wasn't all that sure. Then, as if Caden wanted to change the subject, he looked over at Dalton. "Getting back to what Jace said earlier, I agree with him. It's not all about you, Dalton. One day you're going to find that out."

Dalton rolled his eyes. "I doubt it. Unlike the two of you, I'm responsible in the bedroom."

\#

"Marriage agrees with you."

A smile curved Carson's lips. "Thanks, Roland. I will have to agree with you," she said, after taking a sip of her hot tea. "Sheppard is the best thing to ever happen to me."

"And it shows. I'm happy for you."

She knew he meant it and appreciated it. She appreciated him as well as their friendship. It had been over fifteen years since Becca's death and she often wondered if Roland would ever allow himself to meet someone and fall in love again. The Becca that Carson knew would have wanted him to enjoy life and move on without her, which is something Roland hadn't done.

"Thanks, Roland. Still, I want you to be happy too. Becca would want that for you. Do you ever intend to date?"

She saw the way his chin tightened. "I do date."

She chuckled. "Not seriously."

He didn't say anything for a minute. "No, not seriously and I doubt I will. Ever."

"Ever is a long time."

He stared at her for a moment. "I know, Carson. But I doubt I could love another woman the way I loved Becca."

"You'll never know if you don't open yourself up to meet someone. Isn't that what you told me countless times when I had stopped dating? I listened and met Sheppard."

A half smile curved his lips. "Yes, but I believe it was destined for you and Sheppard to meet and get together. Personally, I like my life just the way it is. A part of me died the night Becca drew her last breath. Now I'm married to Summers Securities and I'm happy about it."

An hour later, while sitting at the desk in her office, Carson couldn't get her conversation with Roland out of her mind. She knew that happily married people felt that everyone should have what they had. But more than anything, she had to be respectful of Roland's feelings. She knew how much he'd loved Becca and that he blamed himself for her death. He believed that if she hadn't been so adamant about freeing him from jail, she'd likely still be alive. He had told Carson more than once that he'd gladly served the fifteen years he'd been given if it would have kept his wife alive.

Carson drew in a deep breath and was about to open the file on her desk when her secretary beeped her on the intercom. "Yes, Ruby?"

"There's a gentleman here to see you, Ms. Granger."

Carson lifted a brow. She didn't have any scheduled appointments for today. "Who is it?"

"Pence Denmark. He says it's imperative that he speak with you."

Blood rushed to Carson's head and everything around her began to swirl. Pence was here? In Charlottesville? Why?

She drew in a deep breath, clearly remembering the last hateful words he'd said to her in the hospital room that day. It didn't matter how many years had passed since then. There were some things a woman just couldn't forget. Especially a woman mourning the death of her child.

What was so important it had brought him all the way from Tampa?

"Ms. Granger?"

Carson stood up from her desk, her spine ramrod straight. He might have caused her pain years ago, but he could never hurt her again. "Yes, Ruby. Please send him in."

16

When the door opened and her ex-husband walked in, Carson sized up the man who'd once made her life a living hell. Although years had passed, the images she remembered darkened her spirit. She wished they wouldn't, but she couldn't help it.

Except for the brush of gray along his temple, the winkles beneath his eyes and the extra weight around his middle, Pence basically looked the same. She would have recognized him if she'd run into him anywhere. But she hadn't run into him anywhere. He'd come here. Why?

"Pence? Why are you in Charlottesville?" she asked, deciding to dispense with formalities. There was no need to shake hands. Or tell each other how long it had been. They both knew. Their divorce hadn't exactly been nasty but it had definitely left a bad taste in her mouth. She'd initiated it. He hadn't fought it. But all through the proceedings, he had been cruel.

"I thought I'd come and let you know in person that Mom passed away two weeks ago."

Carson's anger evaporated and was immediately replaced with pain. She fought to remain standing. "Emma died? How?"

"In her sleep. Doctors think it was a heart attack. She'd never been the same after Dad died."

His father, Stanley, had passed away around ten years ago. He and his wife had been close, nearly inseparable, during the forty-plus years of their marriage. Although she knew Pence wished otherwise, Emma would call her from time to time. And Carson would call her back. The last time they'd talked was about six months ago. Carson had called Emma on her birthday.

"I'm sorry, Pence. Emma was special to me."

"I know."

Carson fought back the urge to say, *Yes, you knew, so you tried to destroy our relationship.*

"I would have called to let you know, just in case you wanted to attend the services, but I didn't have your phone number or know where you'd moved to when you left Tampa. I only found out when I went through Mom's belongings after the funeral. I found several birthday and holidays cards you'd sent her over the years."

She nodded. "And how did you know to come here?"

"I Googled you. I didn't know you'd gone back to using your maiden name."

"There was no reason for me not to," she said, not caring one way or the other just how he felt about her doing that.

"Congratulations on your marriage, by the way. I hope you're happy."

Carson lifted her chin. "Thanks. I'm very happy."

"I'm glad. I heard about your old man when he made national news. I understand he spent time in jail for killing his wife--"

"Thanks for coming all this way to tell me," she said, interrupting his words. The last thing she intended to do was talk to Pence about Sheppard. "And how's your wife?" she asked, deciding to shift the focus off her marriage and on to his.

He shrugged his shoulders. "I've married twice since you and I split and neither worked out. I guess you can say when it comes to marriages, I'm a failure."

If he was waiting for her to refute his words, then he would be waiting a while. She didn't know about his other marriages but he sure hadn't been much of a husband to her.

"Thanks again for coming all this way--"

"Telling you about Mom isn't the only reason I sought you out, Carson."

Was that bitterness she heard in his voice? That was definitely anger now appearing behind the dark pupils in his eyes. She crossed her arms over her chest. "And what's the other reason?"

"You were named in Mom's will."

Shocked, Carson dropped her hands to her side. "I'm named in her will?"

A snarl curled his lips. "Yes. I was her son, her only child, yet she left you something. But it should be mine."

Carson rubbed a hand across her forehead. "Why would she leave anything to me?"

"You won her over. She liked you and never cared for the other two women I married. She didn't even try to get to know them. She blamed me for the divorce. She blamed me for you losing the baby."

Carson lifted her chin. "She didn't blame you. Nobody blamed you. Your parents just didn't appreciate your lack of empathy at the loss of what would have been their first grandchild, Pence. But you were too selfish, too self-centered to understand that."

Using his hand, he waved her words away. "It doesn't matter now." He pulled a sheet of paper from his jacket. "I need you to sign this," he said offering her the document.

She didn't take it. "What is it?"

"It's a document rejecting claim to everything my mother left you."

Carson frowned. "I'm an attorney, Pence. I would never sign anything without thoroughly reviewing it first.

And what makes you think I would reject anything Emma left me?"

"Because by right, it belongs to me. Besides, the man you married is loaded. You don't need my mother's money."

His words angered her. "Keep your paper, Pence. I'm not signing anything. Give me the name of the attorney handling your mother's estate and I'll contact him to see what this is about."

"I'm telling you what this is about. There's no need to contact him. Like I said, you aren't entitled to anything, Carson."

"Evidently Emma felt differently. Have a nice flight back to Florida, Pence."

He stared at her for a long moment and then after placing the paper back in the pocket of his jacket, he glared at her again. "You think I don't know, don't you?"

"And just what don't I think you know?"

"How you've been taking advantage of my mother over the years, using your influence over her to get your law degree and no telling what else."

Carson frowned. "What are you talking about?"

"While going through Mom's belongings, I found the paperwork about that foundation she set up, just to give you those scholarships for your college and law school."

Carson's heart began pounding painfully in her chest. "You're mistaken."

"No, I'm not. I got the paperwork to prove it, as well as verification from her attorney."

Her head began spinning. What Pence was claiming couldn't be true. Yes, she'd gotten scholarships all through college and law school and yes, they'd come from the same foundation. But there was no way Emma had had anything to do with it. "I filled out the forms and applied for the scholarships just like everybody else and--"

"You would have gotten them regardless, and you know it. You used my mother to fund your education and now you think I'm going sit by and let you get your hands on money that should be mine. Well, that won't be happening. Sign the document and give me what's rightfully mine or else."

Carson narrowed her gaze at him. "Or else, what?"

"Or else I'll let everyone know how you milked money out of my poor mother, deliberately taking advantage of her and using her the way you did. I understand that since your husband got released from jail after being found innocent, he's become something of a hero, even being on television doing talk-shows and all. He's regained his family's favorable reputation. I would hate for them to be embroiled in a nasty scandal because of you."

"What kind of a scandal?"

"The one where I tell everyone about how you took advantage of my mother by taking her money, and now you're after your husband's money. I understand that he's a lot older than you. I could say that the only reason you married him was for his wealth."

Carson tried controlling her anger. "How dare you imply something like that?"

"I dare and I will. Unless, you sign this," he said, pulling the document from his jacket again and shoving it at her. "I will let everyone in this town know just what a heartless little gold digger you are."

She glared at him and refused to look at the paper in his hands. "Shove that up your ass, Pence, because I'm not signing it."

"When I finish with you, Carson, even your old man will question the reason you married him."

She lifted her chin. "You don't know my husband."

"Don't need to." He put the paper back into his jacket. "You have twenty-four hours." He pulled out a card and left it on her desk. "You can reach me at this number when you're ready to sign."

"Get the hell out of here Pence, and don't come back."

He stood. "You're making a mistake."

"No, you just did. Now get out."

She watched as he stormed out of her office.

#

Sheppard stepped into Canary's Bar and Grill and glanced around. He didn't see the guys and figured they hadn't arrived yet. That was understandable, since he was thirty minutes early.

His first full day at the office had practically flown by. He'd done a lot of reading and had sat in on various department meetings. He hadn't expected the welcome back party the employees had thrown over the lunch hour. It was good seeing all the old staff. Several of those who'd retired had returned today just to see him. It always overwhelmed him how many people who'd worked for him had believed in his innocence.

"Welcome to Canary's," a waiter said, interrupting his thoughts. "Do you want to sit at the bar or would you prefer a table, sir?"

He glanced at the waiter's name tag. "I'd like a table, Morris. I'll be joined by three others in a few minutes."

The young man beamed at being called by name. "Yes, sir. Please follow me."

Some of the young men he'd mentored at both Glenworth and Delvers had worked as servers or waiters at hotels, fast-food chains or restaurants. They'd told him that it would annoy them when customers looked down their nose at them, trying to make them feel inferior. That complaint had stuck with him and now, whenever he dined out, he referred to his waiter or waitress by name. It was a matter of respect.

CAPTIVATED BY LOVE

After being seated, he was tempted to call Carson and tell her how his first full day back at the office had gone. But then he glanced out the window and saw Striker, Quasar and Stonewall crossing the street, walking in sync. These days, the three men were closer than brothers.

Sheppard could recall when things hadn't always been that way. When the three couldn't get along and Striker and Stonewall had even gone so far as to make plans to kill each other. Luckily, one of the other inmates had apprised Sheppard of those plans and he'd intervened. It had taken a lot of time and even a couple of threats before they'd come around. And to see how close their relationship had become over the years filled him with both pride and gratitude. The three of them, along with the twenty-something others he'd helped during his confinement, were doing well. Since being released, all of them were living productive lives, going back to school, earning college degrees and volunteering to give back to their communities. A couple of them had even gone into politics.

Quasar already had a college degree when he arrived at Glenworth. Striker and Stonewall had earned their associate degrees while confined and once they'd gotten released, they had continued their educations. Stonewall had a master's degree in education and Striker had a MBA. He knew, when time permitted, Stonewall sometimes worked as a substitute teacher at various high schools and Striker taught a class or two at the junior college.

Quasar, the youngest of the three by a year, spent his free time--when he wasn't chasing after women--doing volunteer work at the youth center in town. Sheppard knew they enjoyed working for Roland's security firm as bodyguards...or protectors, as Striker preferred being called.

He watched them enter the establishment. Sheppard stood to greet them and when they reached his table, they exchanged bear hugs.

"Are we late or were you early, Shep?" Quasar asked grinning.

"I was early," Sheppard said when they all sat down. Quasar had started wearing his hair long and it fell past his shoulders. Long hair wasn't allowed at Glenworth and seeing this new hair style on Quasar took some getting used to.

"So how was your first day back at Granger Aeronautics?" Striker asked, leaning back in his chair.

"It was okay. I still have a lot of material to review. So much has changed since I left."

"That's expected. You were gone fifteen years. That's a long time," Stonewall said.

The waiter came and took their drink order and like Sheppard had done, Striker, Quasar and Stonewall thanked the young man, calling him by name. "So how have you guys been doing?" Sheppard asked after the waiter left.

"So far, so good," Striker said. "I'm going to teach a class at the junior college next semester since our work load is down. Now that the election is over, there aren't any local candidates needing protecting."

"I'm teaching a class as well," Stonewall said, smiling. "It's good to have a second profession."

Quasar didn't say anything for a minute and then he admitted, "I've thought about buying a house. One of those fixer-upper deals to flip later. That will probably take up a lot of my time. It seems everyone's attention is now on the Erickson case."

Sheppard had been keeping up with the news. He was well aware of the federal case against mobster, Murphy Erickson. The trial was to start after the holidays and it was anyone's guess how long it would last. Jury selection was underway and he'd heard those selected might be sequestered anywhere from six to twelve weeks.

Erickson was reputed to be the leader of an organized crime ring. Over the past three years, he'd been implicated in over a dozen deaths. He was arrested a year and a half ago and it had taken all this time for the federal prosecutors to build up their case to present to a jury.

"I've been keeping up with that. Although I believe a man is innocent until proven guilty, I hear the Feds have a strong case. They don't intend to let him walk," Sheppard said.

"I heard that as well," Striker said. He paused a moment and then changed the subject. "Anyone heard from Drew lately?"

Andrew Logan was another one of the guys who'd served time at Glenworth with them. He'd started his life of crime at the age of ten, when stealing had become his favorite pastime. Youth detention centers had practically become his second home. Now Andrew had a master's degree in criminal justice and worked on the right side of the law as a police detective in Alexandria.

"Yes, he called me earlier in the week to see how I was doing," Sheppard said, trying to decide who had given him the most trouble, Andrew or Matthew Fontane. Though getting through to them had nearly killed him, he'd refused to give up on either of them.

The table got quiet when Morris delivered their beers. When he left Quasar asked about Carson. "How she's doing? It's been a year, right? Didn't you just have an anniversary?"

Sheppard nodded after taking a sip of his beer. "Yes, it was yesterday. I took her to dinner to celebrate. She's doing fine and still running her law firm and doing pro bono work at Delvers."

"I wish I had her energy," Striker said grinning.

The last thing Sheppard wanted to think about was his wife's energy. She claimed she worked hard to keep up with him in the bedroom when it was quite the opposite. They were definitely making up for lost time.

"And speaking of someone else who has a lot of energy, I can't believe your Dalton," Stonewall interjected. "Jules was out of town last weekend working on a case, and we had a card game at his place. I was ready to call it a night around three but these two--" Stonewall indicated

Striker and Quasar, "--were determined to play all night to win their money back."

Sheppard leaned back in his chair as he listened to the good-natured arguing between the three. It felt good being here, sitting across from them, sipping beer, talking and listening while they joked around with each other. He would never forget his time at Glenworth and doubted they would either. That time was in the past now, and like him, they had moved forward. He knew they liked the work they were doing at Summers Security and it sounded like their personal lives were going okay as well. More than anything, he wanted them to find what his sons had--good women to love. Life was short and there was nothing like having a good woman by your side.

"I'm ordering some fries," Stonewall said. "Anybody else wants to place an order?"

All of them knew of Stonewall's love of junk food. In a roundabout way, he was telling them he was placing an order so they would place their own. Because he didn't share.

#

Pence Denmark walked into his hotel room, pulled out his phone and punched in a number. The call was answered on the second ring. Without saying hello, the person said, "You better have good news for me."

A vein throbbed in Pence's temple. He wished he had never borrowed money from Karl Halifax. The interest on the loan was exorbitant and compounded daily. He didn't have the money he claimed he had anymore, nor the money he figured he could get from Carson

How would she react when she learned his mother had left her over a half-million dollars? She'd left him the same amount but as far as he was concerned, he should have gotten it all. He was no longer married to Carson. They had divorced years ago, so there was no reason for her to have been named in the will.

"Things aren't going as easy as I thought they would, Halifax."

"That's your problem, not mine. You're behind in your payment Denmark, and I want my money. Your gambling habit is your business. When you borrow money from me to pay your debts, and you don't pay me back on time, it becomes my business."

"You'll get your money. I just need more time."

"How much time?"

"At least two weeks."

There was a pause. "I'll give you one additional week and that's it."

The phone went dead in Pence's ear.

17

Y ou want to tell me what's bothering you Carson?"

Carson glanced across the table at Sheppard. As planned, they had met for dinner at Fleurie's. This was one of her favorite restaurants and as usual, dinner had been wonderful. She had basically cleared her plate and had ordered dessert. However, instead of the wine she usually ordered she had decided on hot tea. The last thing she wanted was for her queasy stomach to return.

She studied Sheppard's features. The lines at the corner of his eyes as well as the firm tightening of his mouth meant he'd picked up on something. She didn't think that she was acting any differently than usual. How could this man know her so well?

Carson knew the answer without even thinking hard about it. Sheppard made it his business to know the people he loved, and her, specifically. They'd shared a connection that went a lot deeper than just the physical, mainly because in the beginning, they'd had to. Being involved with him those five years while he was at Delvers gave them time to forge the kind of relationship that was rock solid and could endure just about anything. They had no secrets from each other. So there was no reason not to tell him what was bothering her.

"Pence came to see me today."

She saw his eyebrows raise in surprise. "Your ex-husband?"

"Yes."

"Why?"

She told him what Pence had said. "I honestly didn't know Emma had established those scholarships for me. Pence's parents weren't exactly wealthy, although I know they had money invested."

"Yet she cared enough for you to do what she did. It's not your fault," he said.

"But Pence is going to try and make it look like it was something I did, like I deliberately took advantage of his mother's kindness. I loved Emma and would never have done that."

"And she evidently loved you. Your ex-husband is an ass who is jealous of the relationship that you and his mother shared."

Carson took a sip of her tea, then admitted, "I called John Davis, the man I remembered as Emma's attorney. He verified what Pence said about the scholarships. He said Emma never wanted me to know what she'd done, but that establishing those scholarships for me was absolutely legal.

Pence might not like it, but there's nothing he can do about it."

"I agree."

"But he will try to make things unpleasant for me. He threatened to cause a scandal, making me out to be a gold digger who took advantage of his mother. He's also threatening to spread the rumor that I only married you for your money."

Sheppard snorted. "He's stupid to think I'd believe something like that."

"I don't think he cares whether you believe it, Sheppard. He wants to smear my name. Some people will believe anything. Even lies."

He put down his fork and reached out, taking her hand in his. "And you think I care about that? If you recall, for fifteen years everyone believed me to be a killer. So trust me when I say, I honestly don't give a damn what people believe."

"But I do, Sheppard. For you. For me. For us. And for our family. Years ago, the Grangers' name took a hit. You've made it respectable again. I don't want someone like Pence destroying it."

She drew in a deep breath and continued. "John Davis also said that Emma had written me a letter that she felt would explain everything. He's sending it to me. I should receive it tomorrow."

"What about Denmark?"

"He's given me twenty-four hours to agree to his terms. I'm just hoping he will come to his senses and return to Tampa. I don't want to see him again."

Sheppard didn't say anything as he cut into his steak. He doubted Denmark was out of the picture. There was a reason he'd come all this way. And he wouldn't go home until he got what he wanted.

Sheppard knew it was time to put his skill as a strategic planner to work. There was no way he would let Pence Denmark hurt Carson again.

#

Pence slowed down the rental car when he reached the entrance to Sutton Hills. "Well, I'll be damned," he muttered, looking across the wooden fence at the elegant family estate. "Looks like Carson has done well for herself," he muttered.

That made him even angrier.

He cut off the engine and rolled down the window to get a better view of the Granger estates. He'd done his research and knew that Sutton Hills encompassed over two hundred acres near the foothills of the Blue Ridge Mountains. It had been a thirty-minute drive from Charlottesville, and he had to grudgingly admit that the land was breathtaking. Looking around, he figured that the estate probably had security cameras, so going down the long, winding driveway wouldn't be the smartest move.

He'd acquired a map of the grounds online and knew an equestrian center was located near the entrance. He could see the roof line of the huge structure from the street. From where he sat in the car, he could even see several horses grazing in the pastures. Hell, he'd always wanted a horse and Carson and her husband owned a dozen or so.

From the map, he knew Sutton Hills was divided into four major plots. There was the main house where Carson and her husband probably lived. The house was a monstrosity and could be seen from the road. The three-story structure was an architectural masterpiece and backed up against Mammoth Lake. Why would anyone need a house that large?

The more Pence sat there and saw all Carson had, the angrier he became, especially when he thought of the scholarship money she'd received from his mother.

His thoughts shifted to Karl Halifax. He'd been warned not to do business with the man, but he'd been so sure that he would win the bet. He would have had enough to pay the man out of his own inheritance, had it not been for Carla. His ex-girlfriend had encouraged him to blow most of his money on foolish stuff she'd wanted. And then when he'd refused to spend any more money on her, she'd left him.

He rubbed his hands down his face. He knew he had a gambling addiction. His mother had known it as well, which was why she'd specifically ordered in her will that his inheritance be doled out in yearly installments. He wouldn't get another payout for a year. What would he do until then?

He knew what he had to do. And God help Carson if she didn't go along with him.

#

"Hello."

"Drew, I hope I'm not calling at a bad time," Sheppard said to Andrew Logan, the man who'd once been a fellow inmate.

He and Carson had finished dinner and were headed home in their individual cars. He could see the taillights of her vehicle a few cars ahead of him as they headed toward the outskirts of the city. When he'd been released from prison, one of the first things he did was go shopping for a car. Unfortunately, Dalton had volunteered to come along. Needless to say, he'd left the dealership with a toy. The two seater Mercedes sports car had taken some getting used to. As far as Sheppard was concerned, it had too much power and not enough room.

"No, Shep, you aren't. Is anything wrong?"

"Not sure." He then told Andrew what Carson had shared with him about Pence Denmark. "I don't think he'll leave town and I want to know all there is about him. I have a feeling he's going to be trouble."

"No problem. I'll put him in the database and see what I come up with. I'll also find out if he's still hanging around in Charlottesville. I'll get back to you tomorrow, okay?"

"Thanks Drew."

"No problem, Shep. Glad to help."

When Sheppard ended the call, he felt a lot better. He didn't know Pence Denmark personally, but what Carson had shared about the man--especially his abusive tendencies--Sheppard preferred that Denmark not go anywhere near his wife.

18

G ood morning, Ruby."

"Good morning, Ms. Granger. A package was delivered to you first thing this morning."

"Thanks." Carson headed for her office, smiling at how Ruby had decorated the reception area for the holidays. Her personal assistant had even put up a Christmas tree. That reminded Carson of all the shopping she had yet to do. At least she'd gotten Zina's gift shipped out to her in Houston. It was hard to believe her goddaughter was five years old now. And Roddran had given birth to twins three years ago. Myles wanted two more children and Roddran thought he was crazy. Carson couldn't wait to see if Myles got what he wanted.

Sitting at her desk, Carson verified the package was the letter she expected from John Davis. An envelope addressed to her was inside, along with other documents. She recognized Emma's handwriting immediately.

Leaning back in her chair, Carson began reading Emma's letter.

CAPTIVATED BY LOVE

Carson,

If you're reading this letter, it means I am no longer among the living. That's okay. Losing Stan was hard and now we are together. I had to make a lot of tough decisions and one of them concerned Pence. They say parents can't decide their children's future and Stan and I didn't try to decide Pence's. But we had hoped that with all we'd given him in life, he would have made better choices. Stan and I knew that Pence's celebrating the loss of your child was the last straw for you. We understood. We were hurt by his actions as well. Until the day I die, I will mourn the loss of my only grandchild. You were the best thing to ever happen to Pence. He might not realize it now but hopefully one day he will. Putting my son behind you and remarrying was the best thing you could have done.

I am proud of you and all that you have accomplished. Due to Pence's jealousy, keeping in touch was difficult. I'm sorry about that. But nothing he did could destroy the bond between us. In my heart, you were the daughter I never had, which brings me to the reason I am writing this letter. I've decided to split the value of all the stock I've accumulated between you and Pence. He's not going to like it and I truly don't care. I refuse to let him do in my death what he did while I was alive--stop me from showing my love for you.

Knowing you as I do, I'm sure you will use the inheritance I'm giving you wisely. I also know Pence will probably raise holy hell about me leaving you anything. I wouldn't be surprised if he protests the will. No matter what, do not give in to him. If you prefer not to keep the inheritance, donate it to your favorite charity.

I know whatever decision you make will be a good one.

Love always,

Emma

Carson wiped the tears from her eyes as she refolded the letter. Emma Denmark had been a woman with a beautiful heart and Carson was thankful for the time her mother-in-law had been a part of her life. The day Carson had been released from the hospital after losing the baby, it had been Stan and Emma, not Pence, who'd come to pick her up. Instead of taking her to the home she shared with Pence, they'd taken her to their house.

Her in-laws had given her the love she needed while mourning the loss of her child. Not once had Pence come by or called. After remaining with Stan and Emma for a couple of weeks, she had returned home long enough to pack her things and stop by an attorney's office to file for a divorce.

Knowing that Emma had established those scholarships to help her get through college and law school was overwhelming. There was no way she could have obtained her degrees without them. She would forever be appreciative of her mother-in-law for believing in her and giving her that support.

She glanced at the other documents and saw the check made payable to her for just over five hundred thousand dollars and couldn't help but cry some more.

She was wiping the tears from her eyes when the buzzer on her desk sounded. She pulled in a deep breath before answering. "Yes, Ruby?"

"Just a reminder of your doctor's appointment today at two o'clock."

She nodded. "Thanks, Ruby."

#

Sheppard glanced at the stack of papers on his desk. It would be another day of reading. Good thing he'd gotten used to doing that very thing while locked up. He was just about to sit down at his desk when there was a knock on the door.

"Come in."

Dalton entered, smiling. "Good morning, Dad."

"Good morning, Dalton. You're in a good mood."

His youngest son shrugged, while grinning profusely. "What can I say? My wife keeps me smiling." Dalton dropped down in the chair near the desk. "I want to run an idea by you before I present it to Jace."

"Okay, what is it?"

"John Castor turned in his resignation this morning. His wife wants to be closer to their kids and grandkids so they're moving to Dallas. He needs to be replaced as soon as possible."

Sheppard knew John Castor was head of the IT department and was one of those employees who'd been hired during the time he was in prison. "Okay, what's the problem?"

"There are several good people who've been here a long time. Like Mike Jones who's celebrating his tenth anniversary with the company next month. But in my opinion, the most qualified person has been here less than two years. It's Percy Johnson."

Sheppard nodded. "I see." And he did. Percy and Dalton had attended the same high school. Although they hadn't been close friends, they had played on the same football teams since middle school. From what Sheppard had been told, Dalton had run into Percy waiting on tables in a nightclub he often frequented. He had been catching up on old times, when Percy mentioned he was having a hard time finding a job, even though he'd recently gotten a degree in computer technology, graduating at the top of his class. Percy had been working during the days at Cullum Meat Plant as a forklift operator and moonlighting at night as a waiter. Before the night was over, Dalton had offered Percy a job at Granger Aeronautics.

Sheppard also knew that due to Percy's attention to detail, he was the one who'd noticed the computers at GA had been hacked. That information had ultimately led to the cracking of his wife's murder case, which had resulted in

Sheppard's release from prison. He had met Percy and thanked him personally during one of his visits to the office.

"The final decision will be Jace's," Dalton added.

"Yes, but as head of security, your opinion will carry a lot of weight. I'm sure Jace will welcome your opinion."

Dalton looked rather skeptical. Sheppard lifted a brow. "Why wouldn't he?"

"Like I said, there are a number of others who've worked here longer," Dalton said.

"It doesn't matter. If Percy Johnson is the most qualified, then he's the person you should recommend. But you need to be ready to outline your points when presenting your case."

Dalton shrugged. "Just so you know, I wanted Jace to get rid of John Castor when it was discovered hackers were under his nose."

Jace had told Sheppard all about it and he knew it had been a bone of contention between his two sons for a few months. "Although John Castor was head of IT, Dalton, his job didn't have him involved in the day-to-day operations on the floor. His role was management. He had men working for him who should have detected something amiss. The only one who noticed anything was Percy. Not Mike Jones and the others. That counts for something. But if I recall, Jace said John did take full responsibility for what happened on his watch."

"And you don't think John Castor should have been fired?"

"No. I think Jace made the right call to leave him in that position. You're head of security. Yet if some deranged person managed to get into our building and cause chaos, I wouldn't think of firing you because you're the one in charge. But I would definitely reprimand those you put in place to protect the entrances to the building. If they'd done their jobs, any problems would have been avoided. It's the same situation with John."

Sheppard leaned back on his desk as he continued. "From what I understand, John demoted a couple of people. He felt they should have discovered that device before Percy noticed it on the computers."

Dalton stood and nodded. "Thanks Dad. That helps." He shoved his hand into the pockets of his dress slacks. "And I enjoyed having breakfast with you this morning."

Sheppard smiled. "Same here, although I'll agree with Jace and Caden about Hannah spoiling you."

Dalton waved off his father's words. "You can't believe everything you hear from those guys. Sometimes I feel like disowning them as brothers."

Sheppard chuckled. "Don't think you can do that unless you also plan to disown me as your father."

"Not on your life," Dalton said quickly. "Now that you're back, I intend to keep you around." He checked his watch. "I've got a staff meeting this morning," he said heading for the door. "I'll talk to you later."

Sheppard had taken the seat behind his desk and picked up a pen to jot down notes while reading when his cell phone went off. He picked it up and answered. "This is Sheppard."

"Shep, this is Drew. I've got that information you wanted."

Sheppard glanced at the clock on his desk. It wasn't ten o'clock yet. "That was fast."

"Only because I solicited the help of a friend who works for the FBI. She did a little digging and uncovered some interesting stuff, one thing in particular that I'm sure you'll want to know."

#

"So, other than the occasional queasy stomach, how have you been?"

Carson smiled at the doctor who was sitting on the stool writing in her chart. "I've been doing fine."

Dr. Fisher then tilted his head and looked at her. "When was your last period, Mrs. Granger?"

Why would he ask her that? What did her period have to do with a stomach virus? "Three years ago. I started menopause early."

"A medical physician told you that?"

"No. I wasn't sexually active and figured that's what was happening to my body. The same thing happened to

213

the aunt who raised me, which is why she couldn't have children. I figured the same thing was happening to me."

"But you never had that self-diagnosis verified?"

Carson shrugged. "No. I felt there was no need. I was definitely not going to complain about not having a period."

The man who'd been her regular physician for years had retired a year ago and she'd put off getting a new one. Why go to the trouble of finding a new doctor when there was nothing wrong?

"I see from the questionnaire that you were pregnant once and miscarried."

As always, whenever the topic of the child she'd lost came up, pain settled around her heart. "Yes. That was years ago. I was in my early twenties when that happened."

She paused and watched as Dr. Fisher went back to perusing her file. "Dr. Fisher?"

He looked up at her. "Yes, Mrs. Granger?"

"Is there a reason you're asking me all these questions?"

"Yes, there is," he said, giving her his full attention. "I just went over the results of your lab work. It seems you're pregnant."

19

Sheppard leaned back in his chair. "And just what did your friend uncover Drew?"

"Pence Denmark has a gambling problem. I'm not sure how much of an inheritance his mother left him but court records show it was set up to be dispensed in yearly installments. Evidently, he went on a shopping spree, blowing this year's money instead of paying his loan shark."

"How much he owes?"

"Close to a hundred grand."

Sheppard whistled through his teeth. "I'm not sure how much Emma Demark left Carson but Pence Denmark wants it. Now I understand why. It sounds like he's desperate," he said.

"Yeah, well, you haven't heard the best part of this story. Of course, there's a loan shark involved who is charging extremely high interest rates. From what I can tell, Denmark is already behind in his payment, which is why he's so frantic for cash. But the big surprise is the name of that loan shark."

"Who is it?"

Halifax."

Sheppard set up straight in his chair. "Karl?"

"Yes."

Sheppard couldn't hold back the expletive that flowed from his lips. "Damn...I was hoping..."

"You tried, Sheppard. But not everyone can be saved."

"I know. I know. But I was hoping."

Karl Halifax had served time with Sheppard in Glenworth, for doing then what he was evidently still doing now. He'd come from a family who made their living as loan sharks. One day, Karl had sent one of his goons to collect on a debt and violence had ensued, resulting in a death. A jury had found Karl partially responsible.

Under any other circumstances, Karl was a nice enough young man. However, no matter how hard Sheppard had tried, he could not get him to consider another profession. The family business was the only one he knew, it made him a lot of money and he didn't see anything wrong with it. He felt that his family was obviously providing a service and they weren't holding a gun to anyone's head to accept their terms.

"I thought Karl was in Mississippi."

"He was for a while," Drew said. "But after a few years, he left and moved to Florida. And another thing, Shep."

"What?"

"Pence Denmark is still in Charlottesville. I checked with the airlines and he cancelled his return ticket. There's no telling how long he intends to stay. You might want to let Carson know."

"I will. Thanks for checking on this for me."

"Glad to do it. If you need anything else, let me know."

"I will and take care, Drew."

Sheppard clicked off the phone and leaned back in his chair. His thoughts again went to Karl. He'd been a few years older than Stonewall, Striker and Quasar, but had gotten into just as much trouble. When he'd left Glenworth, he'd promised Sheppard that he'd try a new profession. Evidently, it hadn't been that easy.

Drawing in a deep breath, Sheppard glanced at his watch. Then he picked up the phone and called Carson. He needed to give her a heads-up that Denmark was still in town.

When the call immediately went to voicemail, he figured she was in court. Deciding not to leave a message, he texted her instead and asked her to call him when she got a minute. The sooner she knew about Denmark, the better.

\#

Carson almost tumbled off the examination table. Dr. Fisher had to jump up to steady her. Concern shone in his eyes. "Mrs. Granger, are you all right?"

Carson drew in a deep breath. "No, I'm not all right. I'm forty-three. Too old to be pregnant. There must be some mistake."

Dr. Fisher went back to the stool. "I'm a general practitioner and not a female specialist, but the results are conclusive. I suggest you seek out an obstetrician immediately. There's one connected to this practice. I can see if she's available to verify what I've told you and answer any questions you might have."

Carson's head was spinning. "Yes. Please. I need to talk to someone about what's obviously a mistake."

"Okay. If you don't mind waiting for a few minutes, I'll see if Dr. Givens can see you."

"Thanks."

Dr. Fisher left her alone and Carson's mind whirled. How could she be pregnant? She was forty-three? She had lost a baby before. Still, according to her obstetrician at the time, over twenty-percent of pregnancies ended in miscarriages and it had no bearing on her ability to conceive again.

But it was almost twenty years later...

She shook her head. Personally, she'd welcome the news, since she always wanted a baby. But her thoughts went to Sheppard. His youngest son would be turning thirty in a year or so. Why would he want to start all over again?

Right now, he joked that they were too old for all the lovemaking they did. There was no doubt in her mind that he would also think they were too old to have a baby.

It seemed like forever before she heard a knock at the door. "Come in."

Another doctor walked in, a woman Carson guessed to be close to her own age. "Mrs. Granger? I'm Dr. Givens," she said, offering Carson her hand for a handshake. "Dr. Fisher asked that I talk to you."

"Yes. I believe he read the test wrong. He thinks I'm pregnant."

The woman smiled. "I went over the test results again and he's right. You are pregnant. That's why you've had a queasy stomach lately."

Carson's head began spinning. "B-but I was going through menopause."

"Dr. Fisher mentioned that's what you believed, which I assume is the reason you stopped using birth control."

"Yes."

Dr. Givens nodded. "The absence of a menstrual cycle can be attributed to a number of things. You've indicated you've never experienced pain in your lower extremities, so I would probably rule out any serious medical condition like amenorrhea. In your case, the three year delay was probably due to some sort of hormonal imbalance. But the bottom line is that you are definitely pregnant."

Carson's hand immediately went to her stomach. She had a baby in there? Sheppard's baby. She looked back at Dr. Givens who was watching her intently. "But I'm forty-three," she implored again.

A smile touched the doctor's lip. "Halle Berry had a baby at forty-seven, Janet Jackson at fifty and Marcia Cross had twins at forty-four. Older women giving birth is not uncommon now."

"But isn't there a risk? Especially since I've miscarried before?"

"In some cases but not all. I would suggest you consult your personal obstetrician for an appointment."

She didn't have a personal obstetrician. "Why didn't I have morning sickness instead of a queasy stomach?"

"Every woman's body is different."

Carson nodded. "How far along am I?"

"According to your blood test, you're already two months along. I take it there have been no physical signs yet?"

She shook her head. "Two months? You're sure?"

The woman nodded. "Yes. I didn't detect any issues in your blood work, but again I would suggest you consult your obstetrician for further tests."

An hour later, Carson was still reeling. Instead of going back to her office, she took the highway to Sutton Hills, needing time to fully absorb her new reality. She was pregnant.

She couldn't stop the tears from streaming down her cheeks. She needed this moment of happiness for herself right now. Later, when the shock of what the doctor had told her wore off, she would tell Sheppard. She only hoped and prayed that unlike Pence, Sheppard would want their baby.

#

"You have to tell him, Carson."

Carson drew in a deep breath. When she'd gotten home, the first person she called was Roddran. When her best friend had started screaming, she'd had to move the phone away from her ear. It had taken a good ten minutes to get Roddran to calm down enough that Carson could let her in on the whole story.

"And I will tell him once the shock wears off. I can't believe it. I honestly can't believe it. I never allowed myself to even think something like this could happen."

"Only because you had convinced yourself you couldn't get pregnant. If you recall, I told you to go to the doctor to be sure."

Yes, Roddran had done that. But she really hadn't thought it necessary. "Sheppard's youngest son is almost thirty. My husband is a grandfather to one and has another grandchild on the way. Starting over in fatherhood is probably the last thing he wants. What if--?"

"Stop it, Carson Boyett Granger. I bet any amount of money that Sheppard will be just as happy as you are. He's nothing like your ex, so get that out your mind."

"I know he's nothing like Pence but still, a baby is something we hadn't counted on. We've never even discussed the possibility."

"That's all the more reason to tell him."

"I will. But right now, he's working on a plan to counteract Pence's foolishness."

"Your husband is a smart man. I'm sure he'll come up with something."

Yes, Sheppard was brilliant. She would never forget the day he and Roddran had finally met. Carson had gotten a special permit for Roddran to accompany her to Delvers. Roddran had liked Sheppard on the spot. "But what if Pence starts spreading lies about me marrying Sheppard for his money? Now that I'm pregnant, there are bound to be people who will think the worst and speculate that the only reason I got pregnant was to make sure that I at least got a Granger heir out of my marriage."

"Don't worry about what people think, Carson. And for you to be doing so makes me think that you are still in shock."

"That's why I need some extra time before telling Sheppard. I have to know this issue with Pence is over. Then I'll feel better about breaking the news."

"Fine, but don't wait too long. A new baby is good news. Besides, if you're already two months along, he might start noticing changes in your body."

Carson drew in a deep breath. "I know. But I'm not ready to tell him yet."

#

Carson pulled herself up in the bed when she heard Sheppard take the stairs at what sounded like two at a time. She'd seen his text message to call him. However, after leaving the doctor's office, she'd needed time to pull herself together.

"Hey, you okay?"

She glanced up and Sheppard stood there, lingering in the doorway with concern etched on his face. Carson couldn't help but appreciate the view. His tie was undone and his suit jacket was thrown over his shoulder. He looked totally sexy and oh-so masculine. More than once Pence had referred to Sheppard as an "old man". In her opinion, Sheppard was in a lot better shape than Pence, physically and mentally. And he was definitely better looking.

She nodded. "Yes, I'm okay."

He moved from the doorway and walked into the room, tossing his jacket across the loveseat. "When you didn't respond to my text, I assumed you'd gotten detained in court," he said, coming to sit beside her on the huge bed.

223

She shook her head. "No, I had a doctor's appointment."

"That's right. How did it go?"

That was the perfect opening to tell him about her pregnancy. But as much as she wanted to share her happiness with him, she needed to deal with it on her own first. "It went okay." Then she quickly changed the subject. "I read your text. You said you had something to tell me?"

"Yes, I do. I wanted to give you a heads-up that Denmark is still in town."

That was the last thing she wanted to hear. "I guess it was too much to hope he would go back to Tampa."

Reaching over, he placed his arms around her and brought her closer to him. "Yes, I guess it was."

She didn't say anything for a minute. Instead she sat there inhaling his sensual scent. It felt good to have his arms wrapped around her. She felt safe, loved and protected. Should she tell him about her pregnancy now? While he was sitting here, holding her so tenderly.

"Sheppard?"

"Umm?"

"I--"

At that moment his cell phone went off. When he just sat there, waiting for her to continue, she lost her nerve. "I think you need to get that."

"It's Ben. I can call him back."

Ben was father to Shana and Jules and was married to Mona, who was a professor at the University of Virginia. Carson was looking forward to this weekend, when she and Sheppard would be going to a Christmas party at the university with the couple. Carson liked Ben and Mona. The four of them often did things together, and Ben and Sheppard enjoyed sharing the role of grandfather to baby Rylan.

"Go ahead and take it. I need to use the bathroom anyway."

He leaned down and brushed a kiss across her lips. "Okay. I'll still be here when you come back."

#

Later that night, after his wife had drifted off to sleep, Sheppard slid from the bed and went downstairs to the study to make a call. For the second night straight, he called Drew.

"Hello?"

"Drew, this is Sheppard. I want to know where Denmark is staying while he's in town."

"I figured you would, so I already got the information. He's staying at the Libertine Hotel."

Sheppard raised a brow. "That hotel is within walking distance of Carson's office."

"I know. I guess he wanted to be close by."

"Another mistake."

"So, what do you plan to do?"

Sheppard then outlined to Drew the plan he'd come up with.

"Hmm, I hope it works, Shep."

Shep drew in a deep breath. "I hope so too."

\#

After ending his call to Sheppard, Andrew Logan paced his living room a few times before finally making a decision. He quickly picked up his phone and punched in a number he knew by heart.

"What's up, Drew?"

"Hey Striker. There's something going on with Shep that I think you all ought to know about…just in case." He then told Striker everything he knew.

"Damn," Striker said, his mouth tightening in a frown. "Shep should have let us handle it. Sounds like the guy needs a good ass whipping."

Andrew chuckled. "And that's probably why he didn't let the three of you handle anything. The only reason I'm giving you a heads-up is to protect Shep. The guy threatened Carson and for that, Shep might be pulling off the kid gloves.

A sparkle shone in Striker's eyes. "You think so?"

"Not really," he said, immediately deflating Striker's excitement. Sheppard Granger was the most unflappable person they knew. It took a lot to get him riled. They should know, since they had all tried his patience more times than not.

"Thanks for letting me know what's going on. I'll tell the others. I bet Shep's sons don't even know."

"Probably not. If Shep thought he could keep everyone out of things, he would."

"Tough," Striker said frowning. "It won't be happening."

20

Pence nervously took a sip of coffee as he checked the clock on the nightstand by the bed. It had been almost twenty-four hours since he'd paid Carson a visit. Her time was up. If she thought he'd been joking about causing problems for her and her new husband, she was definitely mistaken.

He glanced up when he heard the knock on the door. The "Do not disturb" sign should have signaled housekeeping that he didn't want his room cleaned. But he did need clean towels, so he might as well grab a few off the cart.

He went to the door and opened it, then wished he'd glanced through the eyepiece first. Instead of housekeeping, he came face to face with some older dude standing there in a suit. "What do you want?" he asked, annoyed at being disturbed.

"Pence Denmark?"

Pence lifted a brow. Who was this guy who wanted to know? "Why?"

"I'm Sheppard Granger and we need to talk."

Understanding lit up Pence's brain. "Are you thinking you can talk me out of going to the media about your wife and how she took advantage of my mother?" he asked grinning, moving aside to let the guy inside the room. He looked harmless enough. The dude was too well-dressed to think about getting his suit dirty.

"Something like that," the man said, coming inside and glancing around.

"Well, it won't work. That money's mine. If Carson had given it to me when I asked her, there wouldn't be a problem. My mother should not have left her anything in her will."

Sheppard turned around to face the man. "But she did and I'd think you would want to honor your mother's wishes."

"Well, I don't intend to."

"Why? Because of your debts? I know about your gambling tendencies, Denmark."

Pence lifted a brow. Evidently Mr. Rich Guy here had checked up on him. "So you know. Nothing wrong with playing the odds every now and then. You win some and then you lose some. No problem."

"It *is* a problem if you can't pay back your loan."

This guy was really starting to annoy him. "Maybe you ought to mind your own business."

"And maybe you ought to seek help. Gambling addiction is a mental health disorder. I can refer you to--"

"Are you calling me crazy?"

Sheppard casually shrugged his shoulders. "Not really. But you have to admit, showing up at Carson's office and threatening to involve her in a scandal that has no merit is kind of crazy. Nobody forced your mother to set up those scholarships for Carson."

"You don't know that. I saw with my own eyes how she worked her way into my parents' good books. There was nothing they wouldn't do for her. After Dad died, Mom lived on a tight income. Carson had no right to take advantage of her."

"The way you did, you mean?" Sheppard said, getting sick and tired of the man's whining.

"She was my mother. I was entitled to anything she wanted to give me. But look, you're here because you undoubtedly want to protect Carson's reputation. I get that. I understand you got a lot of money. So I figure, if you want to reimburse me for all the money my mother paid toward Carson's education, the money she left her in the will, and a few extra thousand for good measure, I'll go away and not come back. So write me a check for a million and I'll leave town."

Sheppard lifted a brow. "A million?"

"Yes."

"Why? So you can pay off your loan shark? I know all about him, too."

Anger flashed in Pence's eyes. "How do you know so damn much about my business?"

"I investigated you. I know quite a lot about you, in fact."

"Good. Then I guess you know I don't make threats lightly."

"Neither do I. Get your loan shark on the phone."

Pence looked dumbfounded. "Why would I want to do that?"

"Who knows? I might be able to help you out. You never know."

Pence rolled his eyes. "I do know. So unless you're ready to drop a million, this conversation is over."

"I don't think so." Sheppard pulled his cell phone out of the pocket of his suit jacket and punched in three numbers. He placed the call on speaker so Pence could hear.

"This is directory assistance. What city and state?" an automated voice asked.

"Tampa, Florida."

"What listing?"

"Karl Halifax."

"What the hell!" Pence shouted. "Are you crazy?" How did this man know of his connection to Halifax?

Sheppard ignored the man's outburst. "No, I'm not crazy. However, I am on the verge of allowing my anger to take control, which is something you don't want to see."

Directory assistance came on the line again. "You have been texted the number, and if you hold on, we will go ahead and connect you."

"Disconnect that call man."

"No. Like I said, I know a lot about you, Denmark. Maybe I ought to tell your loan shark that you're trying to shake me and my wife down for money just to pay off your loan."

Pence threw his head back and laughed. "You think Halifax gives a fuck? All he wants is his money, paid back with interest. He doesn't give a damn how I get it."

"We'll see."

A rough male voice came on the line. "Hello."

Sheppard turned up the speaker volume of his mobile phone so Pence could clearly hear every word. From the look on Pence's face, it was obvious he was rather nervous. "Karl Halifax?" Sheppard asked.

There was a pause, and then as if operating on the side of caution, the man asked, "Who wants to know?"

"I do. Not sure if you remember me but we served time together at Glenworth some years ago."

"And?" Halifax said, as if he hadn't wanted to be reminded of that time.

"And I'm hoping I can ask a favor of you."

There was a chuckle. "I don't do favors."

"I'm hoping you'll do one for me."

Halifax's chuckle was a little louder than the last. "And just who the hell are you?"

"Sheppard Granger."

There was a pause. "Sheppard Granger?"

"Yes."

There was another pause. And then... "Shep?"

"Yes, Karl, it's me." Sheppard kept his eyes trained on Pence the entire time and saw the look of total surprise on his face.

"What the hell! Damn man, it's been years. At least twelve."

"Yes, it's been a long time."

"I heard they found you innocent, after all."

"Yes. But I was in jail for fifteen years."

"Well, I'm glad you're out. Glenworth was a shithole."

"It wasn't that bad."

Halifax chuckled. "Still the do-gooder, I see."

"Trying."

"So what's going on? What kind of favor you need?"

"I'm here with one of your...ahh...customers. I understand he missed his payment date and might need an extension."

"Who is he?"

"His name is Pence Denmark."

Expletives came through the line. "That dickhead. How did you get mixed up with the likes of him?"

"He's threatening my family."

"Say what? How? Why?"

"Long story. Can you do the favor?"

Pence waved his hand in the air to get Sheppard's attention, not that it had ever left him. "What is it, Denmark?"

"Since he's a good friend, how about getting him to cancel the loan altogether," Denmark said, in a tone that was barely a whisper, a hopeful smile on his face.

Sheppard glared at Pence. "You made the loan and you should pay it."

"What did you say, Shep?"

"Sorry about the interruption, Halifax. Denmark is here and was trying to get me to ask you to cancel the loan altogether."

"That won't be happening."

"I wouldn't ask you to do that, anyway. He made the loan and should pay it, exorbitant fees and all. It was his decision to take it on. Just give him an extension."

"I already gave him one. He got another week."

Sheppard drew in a deep breath. "He needs more time than that. He's broke."

"That doesn't surprise me. He gambles. He loses. And then he comes to me to borrow money to pay his debt. But for you, I will give him an extension. Six months. But I expect my money, paid in full with all the interest he owes. I am a business man, after all. And Shep?"

"Yes?"

"Put Denmark on speakerphone so he can hear my every word."

"He's already listening."

"Good. Hey, Denmark?"

Denmark came a little closer. "Yes, Halifax?" he asked in a somewhat shaky voice.

"Because Shep and I go back a long ways, I'm going to extend the note on your loan another six months. At the end, I want my money with all the interest you owe."

"You'll get it," Denmark said eagerly. Sheppard saw relief in the man's features.

"And Denmark?"

"Yes?"

"Another thing. Shep helped keep me alive while I was in the slammer so I owe him. That's the only reason you're getting this break. Don't know what kind of threats you've made against his family, but drop the shit. If I hear of you causing him any more trouble, I'm going to get my boys to whip your ass so bad, you're going to wish you were dead. Then we'll do a Jimmy Hoffa on you. We'll kill you and get rid of your body so it won't ever be found."

Sheppard saw Denmark's eyes nearly pop out the sockets. "But you don't understand. My mother left his wife a lot of money in her will and--"

"I don't give a damn about that. I'm loyal to my friends and brutal to my enemies. Remember that. Hell, I won't even let my boys work you over. I'll personally blow out your brains myself."

Sheppard saw the look of total fear on the man's face. A part of him felt a little sorry for him, but all he had to do was remember just how badly he'd treated Carson.

"Do we understand each other, Denmark?" Halifax asked.

"Y-y-yes, we understand each other," Pence said, all but stuttering in fear.

"Fine. And Shep, it was good talking to you. Wish you the best, man."

"Thanks."

Sheppard clicked off the phone and stared hard at Denmark. "Stay away from my wife. You had the chance to make her happy and you blew it. Your mother evidently thought highly of her and wanted to help her. So get over it."

He turned to leave, but before opening the door, he glanced over his shoulder. "And seriously, please seek out help for your gambling addiction or you're going to eventually lose everything." Sheppard then walked out the door.

When he reached his car moments later, he pulled out his phone and punched in a number. "Halifax?"

"Hey, Shep, how did I do?"

Sheppard shook his head. "Great, but you might have laid it on too thick. He was shaking when I left. When I called you last night, all I asked you to do was agree to the extension."

"Well, I decided to do more. There was nothing wrong with putting the fear of God in his ass."

"Yes, but threatening to blow his brains out? Did you really have to go there? Don't you think that was going a little too far?"

"No. Although I know you don't approve of what I do, it is a legitimate business. And just so you know, since getting out the slammer, I do things differently. I don't use the violence to collect on the loans like I used to. But Denmark had it coming. He should not have gone after your wife like that."

No, he should not have. "Well, thanks for doing me the favor. And I'm glad you've changed your approach. I don't ever want to hear about you going back to Glenworth."

"Hey, I won't ever go back there. Trust me."

"Good. Take care of yourself."

"You, too."

Sheppard hung up the phone, then checked his watch. It was still early. He would grab a cup of coffee before heading back to the office.

As he pulled his car out of the hotel's parking lot, he didn't notice how the occupants of two cars parked not far away waited until he was no longer in sight before getting out of their vehicles.

#

Pence had just hung up the phone after booking a flight out of Charlottesville when there was a knock at the door. Figuring it was housekeeping for real this time, he crossed the room and snatched the door open. He was startled to see six strangers standing there, glaring at him. Three were dressed in business suits and the other three were wearing jeans and t-shirts.

Before he could ask who they were and what they wanted, one of them practically pushed him aside as all six entered his hotel room. "Wait a damn minute. Who are you?" he asked, backing up when one of them, the one who wore his hair in a ponytail, advanced on him.

"We want you gone. Out of Charlottesville within the hour," one of the suits said.

Pence backed up some more. "Who the hell are you guys? I don't know you."

"But we know you," replied one of the rougher looking characters. "And we know all about the trouble you've been causing Carson."

Pence swallowed. *Christ, did his ex-wife have an army protecting her?* "Granger just left here and I agreed not to bother Carson again."

"And we're going to make sure of it," another guy in a suit…the youngest one…said as he glanced around. "Where's your luggage?"

Pence swallowed again. "In the closet. Why?"

Without answering him, another suit wearing dude went to the closet, got his luggage and all but tossed it on the bed, while the others flung open the dresser drawers and began throwing his belongings into it.

"I'm calling the cops," Pence threatened.

"You can do that, but it will have to be after we kick your ass. Don't tempt us," one of the men snarled. "You mess with Carson, and you mess with us. Remember that."

When they had finished, the tallest of the suit-wearing guys said, "Let's go."

Pence backed up again, nearly flattening himself to the wall. He could feel his body shaking. First he'd been threatened by Halifax and now these six goons. "Go where?"

"We're taking you to the airport."

"But I just made a reservation. My flight doesn't leave until noon."

"That means we're getting you there early," one of the t-shirt wearing guys said. "So move."

Pence thought of making a run for it but figured he wouldn't get far. And he totally believed the six of them would end up kicking his ass, just as they'd threatened. But first, he wanted answers. "Who the hell are you?"

They just stared at him, and then one of the suit-wearing men spoke up. "Enemies of yours."

"And just so you know," one of the other guys continued. "There are more than twenty of us ready to protect Shep and Carson from scum like you. If you ever think about returning to make trouble, we'll make you wish you hadn't."

"Let's go," one of the others said. "You're getting a free ride to the airport."

Less than an hour later, Jace, Caden, Dalton, along with Striker, Quasar and Stonewall stood in the parking lot of the airport and watched as Pence Denmark all but ran inside the terminal without looking back.

"You think we've seen the last of him?" Jace asked, still feeling the fury that had overwhelmed him when Striker had contacted him that morning to let him know what was going on. He hadn't been surprised that his father had intended to handle things himself. But Jace would be damned if he'd let some lowlife like Pence Denmark cause problems for his father and the woman he loved.

"It better be the last," Caden all but growled.

"I think it will be," Dalton said. "After that stunt we just pulled, he would be crazy to come back."

"It might have been a stunt for you three, but it was the real deal for me," Stonewall said, drawing in an angry breath. "I was ready to kick his ass all over town."

"So were we," Striker and Quasar said simultaneously.

"Is that why he looked a little pained when he climbed out of the backseat with you, Striker?"

Striker grinned. "It wasn't my fault Stonewall's car is so small that every time he turned a corner, my elbow accidently jabbed the bastard in the ribs."

Jace shook his head, fighting a grin. "Well, I'm glad he's gone." He tried reining in his anger now that Pence was on his way back to where he'd come from. After everything his father had gone through over the years…being locked up for a crime he hadn't committed, separated from his family, and his name dragged through mud…there was no way in hell Jace would have allowed someone like Pence Denmark to waltz in and hurt his father and the woman who loved him, the one who'd waited for him five long years, the woman who made him happy. And if anyone deserved to be happy, it was Sheppard Granger.

Jace checked his watch. "Come on guys, let's go grab some breakfast."

"Sounds like a deal," Striker said.

"Being a bad guy has worked up my appetite," Caden said grinning.

"Mine, too," Quasar chimed in.

"Shit man, you're always hungry," Dalton teased.

"So are you," Stonewall added.

The six men turned and walked back to their parked cars.

21

On her way home Carson thought about the text message she'd gotten from Sheppard. All it had said was – **Denmark has left town. Won't bother us again**.

She'd wanted more details, but when she'd called his mobile phone, it had immediately gone to voicemail. She'd called his office number only to be told that he was in a meeting that would probably last the rest of the day.

After that, they'd basically played phone tag all day. When she'd finally left the courtroom, she'd checked her phone and saw the most recent text message...**Be ready for a night of fun. SG style**. As far as she was concerned, anything they did Sheppard Granger-style was going to be really, really good. This was day two and she still hadn't told him about her pregnancy. Now that Pence had been dealt with—and she wanted to know exactly how that had happened--all she had to worry about was the best way to break the news to Sheppard that he was going to be a father...again.

However, for now she needed to know what happened with Pence. She knew Sheppard had intended to visit her ex-husband this morning but hadn't told her how he was going to handle the meeting. She couldn't see Pence agreeing to leave town on his own. So what kind of pressure had Sheppard used to influence him?

Carson had showered and taken a power nap before Sheppard arrived. As soon as she heard him enter the house, she walked down the stairs. A smile touched her lips when she saw the huge vase of red roses Sheppard carried in his hands. "Are those for me?" she asked excitedly.

"Of course. They are for the woman who captured my heart," Sheppard said handing her the vase.

She sat them on the sofa table, leaning over to inhale their lovely scent. Roses still were her favorite flower and while incarcerated, Sheppard would send them to her a lot. She glanced at him and saw him eyeing her outfit, a short printed caftan. She had worn this particular outfit because she knew he liked her wearing anything that showed her thighs. He was definitely a thigh man.

"What's the occasion, Sheppard? We celebrated our anniversary a few days ago."

"No occasion. Just because I felt like it."

Leaning up on her tip-toes, she brushed a kiss across his lips. "Thanks."

He wrapped his arms around her and pulled her close. "I think you can do better than that, Mrs. Granger."

He then lowered his head and sank his mouth into hers while his hands lowered to her thighs, rubbing his palms over her skin. She wondered at what point he would notice she wasn't wearing underwear.

When he slid his tongue into her mouth and began devouring her, all the wanton need and heated desire that had begun sizzling through her from the moment she'd read his text message was like a jagged edge, cutting passion into her body. This is what she liked the most--the intimacy they shared, the desire to communicate their love this way.

He could ignite sexual feelings inside of her so easily, making sparks of sexual excitement flash through her stomach. The sinfully erotic movements of his hips that made her feel his hard erection poking into her middle brought her right to the edge of sanity. And when he deepened the kiss, an intense throbbing rushed through her entire system.

From the first, she had felt this primal need for him in every part of her body. Even now, her senses were being overwhelmed by him. Still, they needed to talk. She needed to know what happened earlier today with Pence. But at that moment, the only thing on her mind was finding the nearest bed.

Her husband evidently had other ideas when he picked her up and headed for the sofa. In all honestly, she really didn't care what sort of cushion hit her back as long as the ending result would be same. She needed him inside of her. But she had a feeling he would sexually torture her before that happened.

He placed her down and she stretched out on the sofa. Looking up at him, she felt the heat between her legs. Just a look from him could do that to her. Make her sizzle and stir a yearning inside of her. Sometimes, when he stared at her the way he was doing now, he could even make her come. Just from the intensity of his gaze.

"Are you going to stand there and stare or are you going to undress me?" she asked. Carson could actually feel the penetrating fire from his gaze scorch her nipples, heat her belly and singe the area between her legs.

"I want to stare for a minute longer," he said in a sinfully erotic voice.

She wondered if he was noticing any changes in her body. "You can't see anything."

A corner of his lips twitched in a smile. "Trust me, I see plenty."

"Claiming x-ray vision, are you?"

He chuckled. "No, these are the eyes of a man who has a vivid imagination when it comes to his wife."

Her body shifted a little, lifting a leg to deliberately flash him. She was certain he saw that she wasn't wearing any panties. "Why imagine when you can get a first-hand view?"

He shrugged his massive shoulders. For his age, she thought he had an impressive physique. Not that she considered him old, just older. His ingrained charisma, sophistication and suave nature were such a turn-on. He hadn't even removed his business jacket yet and she was already hot for him. "Because imagining what you might or might not have on under that dress is more captivating."

"For me, captivating is what I feel whenever you're inside of me, Sheppard."

She watched the impact of her words on him--the flaring of his nostrils, the penetrating heat of his gaze and the swelling of his erection beneath his pants.

"That can be arranged," he said in a deep, husky voice.

She watched as he began removing his clothes, first his suit jacket and then his shirt. When he tossed both aside and she got a full view of chest, she delighted in how well-built he was. He took physical fitness to heart and had always worked out in prison. One of the things they'd added when they remodeled this house, which had been his grandparents' home, was a fitness room in the basement, as part of his man-cave. She knew he got up early most mornings and worked out. And more than once, she had gotten up and looked out the window to see him jogging down the long lane that led to the main road. He had the stamina of a much younger man and at times, she had a hard time keeping up with him.

While her mind had been occupied, he'd removed his shoes and socks and was now easing down his zipper. This was her favorite part, when he exposed himself. She loved seeing him. She loved taking that part of him in her hands, rubbing her fingers all over it, feeling the strength, the hardness.

"Your breathing is changing, baby. It sounds choppy. Labored. Forced."

He was beginning to toy with her. He knew the reason her breathing was out of whack. "Does it?"

"I think so."

Two could play his game, she thought, shifting her leg to flash him again. His gaze followed the movement and she immediately noticed his breathing change. "Now, from the sound of it, so does yours," she added with a grin.

"You play, you pay," he said, easing his pants down firm, muscular thighs.

"And I have no problem with that," she responded as the throbbing grew more intense between her legs. "You do things to me, Mr. Granger."

"Do I?"

"Yes, you do."

He was standing before her, completely naked. Seeing her husband like this always stroked a primal need within her. He was hairy and she loved the sight and feel of the hair on his chest, legs and definitely between his legs where his huge erection was jutting proudly from a dark thatch of curls.

She knew the shape and fullness of his shaft, so thick and engorged, and how well it would fit snug in her mouth. She would have a licking good time while her fingers skimmed the base of his testicles, feeling his huge and swollen member grow even larger in her mouth.

The first time they'd made love, she had stamped ownership of his shaft. And as far as she was concerned, it had the name Carson written all over it. There was never a time when they made love that she wasn't reminded that special part of him belonged to her.

"Now to get you naked, Carson," he said, moving toward the sofa.

There was just something blatantly sensuous about the way he said her name right before he was about to strip her naked. Then there was the tilt of his chin whenever he touched her. Some would call it an arrogant tilt but she thought of it as a determined one. He intended to give her more pleasure than any woman could possibly endure.

The caftan came off easily. Of course she was completely naked underneath and figured there was no way he hadn't known that. Before tossing the caftan aside, he buried his face in it, as if absorbing her scent from the material through his nostrils. Watching him made her stomach quiver in anticipation.

Then, he leaned down toward her mouth, immediately taking it in his and kissing her with a hunger she felt all the way to her toes. She pulled her naked body up to his, rubbing her breasts against his hairy chest and making intense desire shoot through her veins. He cupped her thighs and then his calloused hands began caressing her while an intense need nearly had her tumbling over the edge.

He released her mouth. "Do you have any idea just how much I love you Carson?" he asked, his voice deep and ragged.

"No. Tell me how much." She knew, but wanted him to tell her anyway.

He looked deep into her eyes. "Today I will show you."

He joined their mouths again and she immediately felt the heat of his desire, the fire behind his words. This kiss was more intimate than the last, more passionate. Blood surged through her veins, the moisture between her legs increased and her pulse was beating like crazy.

He suddenly ended the kiss, then lowered her back to the sofa, spreading her legs in the process. Before she could draw her next breath, he buried his head between them and with unerring ease of a man who knew what he wanted, he slid his tongue between the folds of her feminine mound.

Lordy. There was just something about the feel of having Sheppard's tongue inside her. She began breathing hard as he lapped up her juices in a way that made every nerve in her body, every single cell and molecule, ignite. Intense heat curled inside of her, especially down there.

It only took a few more licks to dismantle her senses, cause her nerves to begin dancing. Then she felt it. What started as a slow stirring began taking over her body and escalating as frissons of fire when he continued to make her his meal. When he pressed his mouth deeper, tilting her thigh at an angle to allow his tongue to gain even greater penetration, she felt a climax building within her.

Sensation after sensation battered her, making her brain sizzle. The very air she was breathing grew thick. Suddenly, a gigantic explosion ripped through her, and it was as if her body was lifted on a higher plane. She arched her back, and he held her, his mouth firmly planted to her feminine mound. Surrendering, she gave herself up to the orgasm rocking through her. Fierce emotions shook her to the core and she tightened her hold on his shoulders.

And that's when she screamed at the top of her lungs.

22

Sheppard always loved hearing his wife scream whenever she was in the throes of an orgasm. Knowing he'd delivered such pleasure made his chest swell. Giving her one last lick, he pulled his mouth away and ran his tongue over his lips to enjoy her lingering taste.

He then eased up her body and she wrapped her arms around him. Their mouths joined and began mating with raw, primitive need. He loved this woman, who had brought so much happiness into his life.

Releasing her mouth, he began licking her jaw and neck, moving toward her chest. Her nipples, turgid and stiff were calling out to him to taste them, suck them, lick all around them.

"Open your legs for me, Carson," he whispered huskily.

The moment she did so, he planted the fullness of his erection at the entrance of her feminine folds. He stared down at her, seeing aroused eyes look back at him. "I love you," he whispered.

"I love you, too," she whispered back. "For always."

Her words were like a torch that had been lit, and the love and desire he saw in her eyes pushed him over. He eased inside of her, inch by inch, loving how her inner muscles clenched him hard. The force of her body gripping his was driving him insane, making him push into her deeper, needing to get as buried inside of her as he could go.

He could feel her fingers dig into his shoulder blades. There was no pain, only the torture of wanting her.

Sheppard began moving, easing in and out of her, loving the sound she made when he did, loving the way her scent filled the room. He continued to gaze down at her, watching how the heat of desire in her eyes burned right into him. He felt all the passion neither of them could hold back. Unrestrained and unlimited.

Their mating became more ravenous and he couldn't hold back a groan. His hips kept pounding into her, thrusting hard with relentless speed, unwavering desire. He tilted his head and then lowered it to capture her mouth. He needed to kiss her, mingle their tongues, and entwine their minds.

And then it happened.

It was as if the entire house shook the moment an orgasm rammed through their bodies. He continued to thrust into her with long, hard and powerful strokes. A part of him wished he could keep her like this, pinned beneath his body, for eternity.

The force of their pleasure pushed him over the edge and he took her right with him. She screamed again and the sound make his body jerk in a succession of orgasmic strikes. His hands moved all over her body, needing to touch her skin, feel her heat. Intense pleasure rocked through his veins and made him call out her name in a guttural growl.

He lowered his face to settle in the area between her breasts, drawing in the scent of her, of them, through his nostrils. This was the kind of lovemaking they shared. The kind that blew his mind, and connected them in both a physical and mental way. This kind of intimate connection was all theirs. It would always be theirs. She tilted her head up and offered her mouth. He took it, devouring her in a kiss that he felt all the way to his soul.

He snatched his mouth away when another orgasm ripped through him and he roared out his pleasure when she screamed hers. And he knew tonight was just the beginning of another hot and steamy Sheppard and Carson weekend.

#

"We're definitely getting too old for this."

Carson barely found the strength to move. If he thought they were too old for this, then how would he feel about them becoming parents? Would he think they were too old for that, as well? She tried pushing the thought to the back of her mind and instead concentrated on how he'd made her feel.

After no telling how many back to back orgasms they'd had, they were lying there, facing each other, their limbs entwined. Their bodies were slick from sweat and their breathing choppy. She wondered at what point her body would begin feeling normal again and not a mass of ecstatic sensations.

At some point, she couldn't rightly remember when, they'd made it upstairs to the bedroom after making love on the sofa and in front of the fireplace. There was nothing like seeing the heat of a blaze while stoking your own fire.

"Hungry?"

She somehow found the strength to tilt her head to look over at Sheppard. Yes, she was hungry. They had definitely worked up an appetite and she felt giddy in knowing she was eating for two. He glanced over at the clock. They'd been going at it for four hours. It was a good thing Dr. Givens had assured her that she didn't have to decrease her sexual activities due to her pregnancy. "Yes, but I doubt if I can make it downstairs to the kitchen even if I wanted to."

He brushed a kiss across her lips. "You don't have to. I'll scramble up something and bring it to you."

She knew he was being modest. He was a good cook. Usually whenever he was in the kitchen, she would help out. But before he left her side, they needed to talk. "Tell me what happened with Pence, Sheppard."

"Okay."

He began talking, telling her of his call to Andrew Logan and the information Andrew had provided to him. It didn't surprise her about Pence's gambling addiction. While they'd been married, he'd played Lotto like all those numbers were going out of style. He never won anything big but had succeeded in gaining enough to make him want to try again.

"Are you saying that the man who was his loan shark was someone you'd mentored at Glenworth?" she asked him, amazed.

"Yes. Talk about a coincidence. But I never managed to get through to Karl Halifax, no matter how hard I tried. He'd come from a family of loan sharks and that was the life he knew. Before leaving Glenworth, Halifax and I had a long talk. Although he never said he would get out the business, I had hoped."

"You can't change everyone, Sheppard," she said softly.

"I know, but I think I could have, if I'd had more time with Halifax. Unfortunately, when I arrived at Glenworth, he was on the last leg of his sentence."

He paused a minute, shaking his head at the lost opportunity. Then he continued. "I contacted Halifax and he and I came up with a plan. As a favor to me, he agreed to an extension of Pence's loan and went further and told him not to come back and bother us again."

"And you don't think Pence will?"

255

Sheppard shifted in bed to bring her body even closer to his. "Halifax comes across as a bad-ass, and my guess is that the men who work for him do so as well. Halifax's threats were convincing enough. Let's just say he went above and beyond what I asked him to do. Poor Pence was shaking in his shoes. I kind of felt sorry for him. But when I thought of how he'd talked to my wife, I pushed my empathy aside." He smiled gently at her.

"What I hadn't counted on was Drew telling Striker about what I was doing. Striker passed on the news to Quasar and Stonewall as well as to my sons. The six of them showed up at the hotel where Pence was staying after I left. I hadn't known they'd paid him a visit until later today when they told me about it."

Carson raised up on her elbow with widened eyes. "The six of them went to see Pence?"

"Yes. It's a good thing Roland is out of town or I have a feeling he would have gone with them, too. They're all very protective of you, sweetheart."

She knew what Sheppard said was true. There had always been a close relationship between her and Roland. And since marrying Sheppard, his sons and the men he considered surrogate sons, had accepted her as a part of his life as well. "What happened?"

"From what I understand, they added to Halifax's threats and really put the fear of God into Pence. They even made sure he got to the airport, whether he wanted to go or not. Took him there themselves."

Carson didn't want to smile but she couldn't help it. She'd accepted that her ex-husband was the worst kind of bully. He could dish it out but couldn't take it. She knew how protective Sheppard's sons—real and surrogate--were of him. If they felt the need to show up at Pence's hotel, she had a feeling the scene hadn't been pretty.

"Well, I'm glad he's gone. I intend to put all the money Emma left me to good use by donating it to your foundation."

Surprise showed in his eyes. "You don't have to do that."

"I want to do it, Sheppard. And the day you decide to switch your focus from Granger Aeronautics to your foundation full-time, I want to join you."

He lifted a brow. "You do?"

"Yes. There are so many young people out there who need us. If we can reach them before they make it into the criminal system, just imagine how many lives we'd be changing."

Sheppard pulled her into his arms, burying his face in the side of her neck. She knew what she'd just offered to do had touched him deeply. She figured that knowing the woman he loved also shared his dream undoubtedly meant a lot to him.

"I love you, baby."

"And I love you, too, Sheppard."

And then she leaned in and lowered her mouth to his.

23

"A re you ready to tell me what's been bothering you for the past few days?" Sheppard asked Carson as they walked into their home after attending the Christmas party at the university with Ben and Mona.

Carson thought it had been a fun night, filled with holiday cheer, good food and dancing. It was hard to believe that a little more than a year ago, Mona had been blind, not sure if she would get back her eyesight. And Ben had fallen in love with her, not caring if she did or not. Now the couple were married, Mona had her sight back and she knew the couple, like her and Sheppard, intended to share the rest of their lives together. The only difference was that unknowing to Sheppard, his life would be changing in less than nine months.

She swallowed as she placed her clutch bag on the table. "What makes you think something is bothering me?"

He shrugged his shoulders. "You've seemed preoccupied about something lately."

She wished he couldn't read her so well. Four days had passed since being told she was pregnant and she hadn't worked up the nerve to tell Sheppard yet. "I'm fine, Sheppard."

She decided to ask him a question while making an observation. "Caden and Shiloh looked cheerful this morning when they joined us for breakfast. You can tell they're happy about the baby."

A huge smile touched Sheppard's lips. "Yes, they are and I'm happy for them. I've always known those two would eventually get together. They were inseparable as kids. I'm glad they were able to work out whatever issues were keeping them apart. And now they're happily married with a baby on the way. Another grandchild for me. For us."

She swallowed. Why couldn't he see them as something other than grandparents? Did the possibility of a child of their own ever cross his mind? She fought back tears. Too late, one slipped from her eyes. She tried to quickly swipe it away.

"Carson? Sweetheart? What's wrong?"

Instead of answering him, she turned and raced up the stairs.

#

What the hell? Sheppard took the stairs two at a time after her, wondering what had upset Carson. Why had she raced off that way? He was so attuned to her that he had picked up on the fact that lately, her mind definitely seemed to be somewhere else. Had he misjudged Pence Denmark? Had the man contacted her again? Was he threatening her? The very thought that could be a possibility filled him with anger.

He opened the door and found her in the middle of their room, undressing. "Carson, what's wrong? And don't tell me you're fine, because you're not," he said in a voice firmer than what he'd meant for it to be.

When she grabbed for her bathrobe as if to cover herself, he raised a brow. Why was she acting so shy? It wasn't as if he hadn't seen her naked before.

She turned to him as she belted the sash of the robe around her waist. "I am fine, Sheppard."

He wondered how she could claim such a thing when it was obvious she'd been crying. Instead of saying anything, he crossed the room and swept her into his arms, then carried her over to the loveseat and cradled her in his lap.

He held her and she smothered her face into his chest and cried, openly and brokenly. The sound tore at his heart and he tightened his hold on her. "Baby, what's wrong?" he whispered close to her ear, about to come apart himself at seeing her so broken up. "Talk to me, Carson. Tell me what's wrong. Is it Denmark? Did he contact you again? Is he back in Charlottesville?"

She snatched her face away from his chest and looked up at him with startled, teary eyes. "No! It's not Pence."

He was glad to hear that, but there was definitely something wrong. What wasn't she telling him? "Do you remember when we decided to become involved, Carson?"

She nodded and he wondered if she was aware that tears were still falling from her eyes. "Yes."

"We made a pact that nothing would ever come between us. That there was nothing we couldn't confront together. Do you recall us doing that, sweetheart?"

She nodded again and swiped at the tears. "Yes, I remember."

Deciding to help, he pulled a handkerchief from his pocket and gently wiped them away. "Are you going to back out on your promise to me? Our promise to each other, Carson?"

She swallowed and then said softly. "I don't want to."

He held her gaze. "Why do you feel the need to even think that you have to?"

"It's sort of complicated."

He reached out and wiped another tear from her eyes. "Nothing is too complicated for Sheppard and Carson Granger to handle. If the two of us indulging in an affair for five years while I was locked up wasn't complicated, then as far as I'm concerned, nothing is."

She didn't say anything for a minute, then she took a deep breath. "I went to the doctor a few days ago, remember?"

"Yes, and you said it went okay."

"Yes, I told you that because I wasn't ready to tell you everything."

Sheppard stiffened. Had it been more than the stomach virus she assumed? Was Carson about to tell him that she was deathly ill or something? Could he handle it if she was? The thought of losing her suddenly took a firm grip of his senses. His emotions. He fought dread from ripping out his insides. He took a deep breath to prepare his mind for whatever she was about to say. "And what weren't you ready to tell me?"

She began to shiver and he tightened his arms around her. "Carson?" What is it? Please tell me, baby."

She met his gaze, holding it for what seemed like a very long time. He watched her lips tremble. "I'm pregnant, Sheppard."

#

Carson stared at her husband. She watched how he blinked a few times, as if to make sure he'd heard her correctly. Then as if he needed to make sure, he asked in a low, incredulous tone. "You're pregnant?"

She nodded. "Yes. I honestly didn't think I could get pregnant. Otherwise, I would have--"

"Pregnant? You're actually having a baby?" he interrupted to asked again.

"Yes."

And then he did the one thing she hadn't expected him to do. He threw his head back and let out a loud whoop. He actually hollered. Did that mean...?

"You don't mind having a baby at our age?"

He laughed and his expression was one of complete happiness. "Oh, so now my beautiful wife, *you* want to the play the age card?"

"No, but I figured me getting pregnant would be the last thing you'd want. You have a son who'll be thirty in another year or so."

"Yes, and I also have a son who's thirty-one and another who will be celebrating his thirty-third birthday in a few months. I also have one grandchild and a second one on the way. What does that have to do with anything?"

"I just assumed you were past the age of wanting to become a father again."

"I honestly hadn't thought about it, since you said you couldn't get pregnant."

She fretted with her hands. "I honestly thought I couldn't. If I'd known, I would have used birth control."

"What about you, Carson. Are you upset about being pregnant because you don't want a baby at forty-three?"

She shook her head. "No, I want a baby. I've always wanted a baby. Granted, I was concerned about being pregnant at my age, but the doctor says it should be okay. I was concerned about how you would handle the news. That's why I delayed telling you."

He lifted a brow. "You actually thought I wouldn't want our baby?"

She shrugged. "You always tease me about us getting old. I wasn't sure what to think."

He smiled tenderly as he brushed a lock of hair away from her face. "Well, let me set the record straight. I am happy about it. Very happy. I want our baby and I intend to be a good father. I will take care of you and our child."

He didn't say anything for a minute. "To be honest, that was the one thing that nearly kept me from getting into a serious relationship with you. When you told me how cruel Denmark was when you lost your baby, all I could think of was that you deserved to be a mother one day, and a child was the one thing I couldn't give you."

He paused a moment and then continued. "I figured that by the time I was eligible for parole, you would be well beyond your childbearing years. And now to know I've given you the one thing I thought I'd never would makes me very happy Carson. I want this baby, our baby, as much as you do. A Granger baby that we've created. How wonderful is that?"

"Oh, Sheppard." She reached up and wrapped her arms around his neck, kissing him with all the love in her heart. When she was about to release his mouth, he took over the kiss and deepened it.

When he finally pulled back, he placed kisses around her lips and asked, "How far along are you?"

She smiled, feeling totally and completely happy. "I'm two months already. Because of my age and my past miscarriage, the doctor will probably want to monitor my progress for a while." She paused. "For that reason, I prefer not announcing my pregnancy until I get past the first trimester."

"You're two months now. I'd think you'll be showing in another month or so."

That was probably true. Now that she knew she was pregnant, she routinely checked her body for changes and noticed some that she hadn't noticed before. "I want to tell your sons and of course, their wives and Hannah. I don't have an obstetrician and want to talk to Shiloh. She loves the doctor she's seeing, which is the same one Shana used when she was pregnant with Rylan. But I'd rather not tell anyone else, right now. Not even Roland and the guys. At least, not until my visit to the doctor. I don't want anyone to worry about me." She knew he was aware that the guys she was referring to were Striker, Quasar and Stonewall.

"Okay, sweetheart," he said, pulling her even closer into his arms. "Anything you want. When do you want to tell the others?"

"They're coming over in the morning for breakfast and to decorate the Christmas tree in the boathouse. Let's tell them then," she said, happily. Hannah wanted to prepare a special pre-Christmas breakfast before leaving to spend the holidays with her daughter in Texas. It would be an intimate breakfast with Sheppard's sons, their wives and Hannah.

"The sooner I can talk to Shiloh and Shana about their obstetrician, the better," she added. "A lot of doctor offices are closing for the holidays and won't reopen until after the first of the year. I want to make an appointment right away so I can be seen right after the holidays."

Sheppard smiled brightly. "I think telling them tomorrow at breakfast is a great idea." He then lowered his mouth to hers.

24

Carson awoke the next morning to find her body practically plastered to Sheppard's. They were both naked and his arm was slung over her waist with the palm of his hand resting on her tummy, as if he needed contact with the baby nestled inside of it.

She smiled, knowing she was truly loved. Over the past six years, Sheppard had told her countless times how much he loved her. He had openly displayed his affections. And now their son or daughter would be living proof of it. Proof of all the love they shared.

Carson had never considered herself a cry baby, but she'd done a lot of crying last night. She even felt misty-eyed this morning. Part of the tears last night had been of apprehension. This morning, they were tears of joy. She was having her husband's baby. Sheppard was happy and so was she. He was everything she could possibly want in a man and a husband. She felt like the luckiest woman in the world.

"You're beautiful in the mornings. In fact, I think you're beautiful every time I look at you, sweetheart."

She glanced over to find Sheppard awake and looking at her. "Thanks." His hand was tenderly caressing her stomach. "Spoiling him or her already?" she teased.

"I might as well and will love every minute doing so. Which do you prefer, a girl or boy?"

She chuckled. "Doesn't matter. Mainly a healthy baby who looks like its father."

Sheppard leaned up and placed a kiss on her lips. "I was hoping it would look like its mother."

"What about you? Which do you prefer?"

"Like you, I'd want a healthy baby." He then glanced over at the clock. "Everyone will start arriving in a few hours for breakfast, so you know what that means, right?"

Carson smiled. Yes, she knew what that meant. It was time for them to engage in some early morning sexual delight, SG style. She shifted in bed and wrapped her arms around his neck. "Yes, I know. Bring it on, Mr. Granger. Bring it on."

#

To begin a new tradition, Hannah suggested they host the pre-Christmas breakfast in the new boathouse and everyone agreed. The place was huge and the architectural design was totally different from the previous one. The new boathouse was only a stone's throw away from the main house and had more guest bedrooms, a game room, a massive party room with a brick fireplace that overlooked Mammoth Lake, a dining area and a spacious kitchen. Hannah had officially christened the kitchen that morning. And she, along with the Granger husbands and wives, had decorated the huge Christmas tree. Sheppard was glad he'd made the decision to tear down the old boathouse and replace it with a new one. They needed to create new memories.

"As usual, breakfast was great, Hannah," Dalton said, hugging the older woman."

"You should know," Caden said grinning. "You ate most of the pancakes. She didn't make them just for you, you know."

"Of course she did," Dalton smirked, dropping down on the sofa next to his wife.

"Feeling entitled again?" Jace asked his youngest brother when he joined his own wife on one of the loveseats.

After breakfast, they had all pitched in to decorate the huge tree. It was beautiful with all the twinkling lights and colorful decorations. After resting up a bit, the men wanted to watch a football game on television and the woman said they intended to go shopping to grab last minute items on their list.

"Of course I feel entitled," Dalton continued, grinning all over himself. "Why wouldn't I?" He then looked over at his father who was standing next to his wife. Carson always seemed to glow like a new bride, which is why he thought the nickname Wedded Bliss suited her.

Dalton thought that a lot had been revealed about his mother during the investigation to free his dad and bring to justice those who'd actually killed his mother. And none of it had been pretty. Maybe that was one of the reasons he liked seeing his father and Carson together. Around Carson, his father seemed to be an extremely happy man and he was happy for him.

"So Dad, you wanted to talk to us?" Jace said, grabbing everyone's attention. Rylan, who'd grown weary of watching the flashing lights on the Christmas tree, was asleep in a portable crib. But Jace knew that wouldn't last long. His son had perfected the art of power naps.

Sheppard left his place at the fireplace and came to stand in front of the group. He glanced around the room at his sons, their wives and Hannah. For as long as he lived, Hannah would always be considered a member of the family.

"First," Sheppard started off by saying, "I want to thank Hannah for such a wonderful breakfast. She didn't have to do it and after all these years, she is still spoiling us."

"Some of us more than others," Caden shouted out, grinning.

"Don't hate, Caden," Dalton shouted back before blowing Hannah a kiss. The older woman merely smiled, pretending to catch his kiss and stuff it in her pocket for safe keeping. It was a gesture she'd perfected through the years with the Granger boys.

Sheppard couldn't help but chuckle at the exchange because everyone knew Dalton blew more kisses Hannah's way than anyone because, not surprisingly, he thought of himself as her favorite. "I have two announcements to make. The first one is that I'll only be working at Granger Aeronautics on a full-time basis for another year."

"Why?" Caden asked before the others could.

Sheppard was prepared for that question and decided to explain things to him the same way he'd explained it to Carson weeks ago. "Dad had planned to retire before I was arrested. Once I was convicted, retirement was no longer an option for him. He worked tirelessly for the next fifteen years to keep the company afloat for me—and for his grandsons."

He paused a moment and seeing he still had everyone's absolute attention, he continued. "Had I returned when Dad assumed I would, then I would be doing the same thing about now. I would be thinking about retiring and leaving the company to my sons."

He turned his attention to his oldest son. "Jace, you're doing a fantastic job as CEO. I know you never thought of it as your legacy, but I believe that deep down, you love GA as much as I once did."

"Once did? Are you saying you no longer love the company?" Caden asked, with a surprised glint in his eyes.

"Not with the passion that I once did," Sheppard said honestly. "My heart is elsewhere, Caden."

"Where?" Dalton asked.

Sheppard paused a minute and drew in a deep breath. "With the Sheppard Granger Foundation for Troubled Teens. I'm needed more there than at Granger Aeronautics."

Nobody said anything. Everyone, especially Jace, Caden and Dalton just sat there, staring at him. Finally, Jace broke the silence. "Thanks Dad, for believing in me enough to feel I can handle the running of GA. I guess I always assumed when you were released from jail, you'd return and run the company. All I want is for you to be happy. If anyone deserves happiness, it's you."

"Thanks, Jace. That's why I'll remain at GA for at least a year. I want to continue to get acclimated to things so I'll be available to help out and be a consultant whenever I'm needed."

He glanced over at his other two sons. "So what do you guys think?"

Caden spoke up. "I agree with Jace, Dad. You deserve to be happy and take on the career you truly want." He reached out and took Shiloh's hand in his. "Because we're having a baby, I intend to stay around home more, which means no more being away on concert tours for a while. And I'm fine with that. I'll be satisfied in putting out an album every now and then. My primary focus is my family, so I'll work alongside Jace anyway I can."

All eyes went to Dalton who only smiled and asked, "What can I say?"

"More than you should," Jace said, getting chuckles from the others in the room.

"Okay," Dalton said. "I won't be the odd ball and say that if Dad can walk away from the company, there's no reason I can't, too. After all, I believe in working smarter, not harder."

"Which means he doesn't believe in working at all," Caden piped in, grinning.

Sheppard was certain that if he and Hannah had not been in the room, Dalton would have told his brothers to kiss off in a not so nice way.

"But the truth of the matter, Dad--" Dalton continued, "--is that I actually like being at GA."

"Note that he said, *being* there and not *working* there," Jace interjected with a chuckle.

Ignoring his oldest brother, Dalton continued. "I enjoy heading up the security department and I've established a good relationship with the men who work for me." He then glanced over at Jace. "And I'm glad you agreed with my suggestion to place Percy Johnson as head of the IP Department. Smart move on your part." Smiling devilishly, he added, "Even smarter on mine for the recommendation." He overlooked Jace and Caden's groans while he took a sip of the hot apple cider.

Dalton then turned to his father. "I don't have a problem with you pursuing the career you want, Dad. I'm just glad you're home. Having you back with us means everything."

Sheppard's chest swelled and deep emotions filled him to the brim. He was so proud of his sons. "Thanks for your understanding guys. And like I said, I'm not going anywhere for a while. I have a good man running things for me at the Foundation and I am okay with that for now."

He then reached out his hand for Carson to join him in the center of the room. She had remained standing by the Christmas tree, giving him center stage. But for this next announcement, he wanted her by his side. He took her hand in his. "Now Carson and I have an announcement to make," Sheppard said smiling even brighter.

"Let me guess," Dalton said. "She's leaving her job as well, to work alongside you at the foundation."

"Something like that," Sheppard said, grinning broadly.

"What is it, Dad?" Jace asked. It looked like he had an idea what the announcement might be and if that was true, he and Caden needed to get ready to pick Dalton up off the floor because there was no way he wouldn't pass out.

"Carson and I are expecting."

All eyes immediately went to Dalton and watched as a confused expression touched his face. "Expecting what?" he asked.

"A baby."

Dalton's mouth dropped. "A baby?"

"Yes."

"A baby?" Dalton asked again.

"Yes."

"A baby?" Dalton asked for a third time.

Sheppard and everyone else in the room wondered how many times Dalton would ask the same question before it finally sank in. "Yes, Dalton, a baby."

Hannah let out a squeal and Jace and Caden and all the wives stood and rushed across the room to congratulate their father and Carson. Dalton continued to sit there, stunned. Finally, the explosion happened when he exclaimed in a loud voice. "What the hell!" And then as expected, he began asking questions.

"How did that happen?" Dalton asked, as if mystified. "Did Carson have a cold like Shana?"

Sheppard lifted a brow. "A cold?"

"Never mind about the cold," Dalton said, waving off his words. "How did this happen?"

The room got quiet. "What part of Reproduction 101 don't you understand, Dalton?" Sheppard asked in a calm tone.

Dalton rolled his eyes. "I know that, but what I don't understand is how it happened to you. Your oldest son has a baby and another son is having one in less than nine months. You're a grandfather, for God's sake. Your youngest son is twenty-nine. Why on earth would you want to start all over with the daddy thing?"

Sheppard smiled, showing his patience for his youngest son's questions and flare for dramatics. "I have no problem starting over with the *daddy thing* because I've created a human being who is a part of me and Carson, and who will be living proof of the love we share. What man wouldn't want that of the woman he loves, Dalton? To know that he's created a life within her body."

He looked over at Carson and smiled. "We're looking forward to expanding the Granger family."

"You want even more babies?" Dalton asked, as if simply shocked at the thought of such a thing.

"That might be a possibility."

"*Jesus,*" Dalton moaned.

"Well I'm happy about it, Dad. Congratulations to you and Carson," Jace said grinning. "Just think, an uncle or aunt that Rylan will play with."

"Same for our child," Caden added happily. "Congratulations, you two. The thought of another younger brother or a sister doesn't bother me, just as long as you keep them away from Dalton. I don't want any of his traits to rub off on an impressionable child."

"You're all missing my point," Dalton said, looking around the room.

"And just what is your point, Dalton?" his wife Jules asked. She had left Carson's side to come stand in front of her husband. She glared at him. "Do you disagree with your father? What man wouldn't want to create a life within the body of the woman he loves, Dalton?"

Dalton rolled his eyes. "You're still missing the point. It's about responsibility in the bedroom."

"Oh," Jules said, thumping her chin with the tip of her finger several times. "Oh, I see. You're saying men don't make mistakes? That they can't get so caught up in the moment that birth control can't be an afterthought? That passion can't take over your mind and make you forget everything?"

Dalton glared at his wife. "Now what's your point?"

Jules tilted her head to look up at him. "The point is, Dalton Richard Granger, that *your* wife is pregnant. So explain that."

The entire room got deathly quiet. It seemed even the logs crackling in the fireplace ceased to make a noise. And had Sheppard imagined it but did the lights on the Christmas tree miss a blink?The look of total and complete shock on his youngest son's face was something he'd never forget, definitely worthy of being a Kodak moment. Caden thought so and pulled out his cell phone and snapped a picture.

Everyone held their breaths, waiting for Dalton's comeback. He finally broke his silence, coming out of his shocked state and asking in a stunned voice, "How? When?"

Jules smiled sweetly. "How? I can tell you that easily." She leaned over and whispered something in her husband's ear. Sheppard wondered what she'd said when he saw Dalton's tight jaw loosen up some.

Jules then leaned away from Dalton and actually winked at him. "And as to when, Dalton..." She again leaned forward and whispered into his ear.

Sheppard stared and watched as his son's eyes widened and then a huge smile touched his lips. He wasn't sure what Jules had reminded Dalton of but evidently the memory was bringing him out of his crazy stupor.

"Hey, no fair," Jace shouted out. "No whispering. We want to know the *how* and *when* as well."

"Mind your own business, Jace," Dalton said before pulling his wife in his arms and kissing her in front of everyone.

When it seemed they'd forgotten they had an audience, Sheppard cleared his throat. Dalton released his wife's mouth. A non-apologetic grin touched his lips. "Sorry about that."

"So tell us, Dalton," Caden asked. "How did Jules get pregnant when you claim Grangers don't get women pregnant? What part of Granddad's birds and the bees lecture did you miss?"

"Kiss it, Caden. I didn't miss any of it. Jules is not just any woman, she's my wife. That's makes a difference."

"So, you're happy about it?" Jules asked her husband.

He smiled down at her. "Yes, I am very happy about it because I know you'll have the ability to take care of our baby and still take care of me. No sweat."

"It's not all about you, Dalton," Jace said, shaking his head. "I can't wait until the baby comes and you find that out."

Sheppard glanced around the room, his heart nearly bursting in his chest at the sight of all the people he loved. They were his family. The Grangers. Even Hannah. He believed that if his father had lived, Richard would have eventually made Hannah his wife.

"I am happy," he said, pulling Carson close to his side. "This will be a special Christmas this year. Three new Grangers have been created. Our legacy lives on."

He then looked down at his wife and knew he was totally and completely captivated by love. Her love.

EPILOGUE

A month later...

This is *Connie Moore reporting live from the Martin Luther King, Jr. Performing Arts Center for the annual I Have A Dream Charity Ball. Everyone in attendance is dressed to the nines and out in large numbers tonight. Mayor Ivan Greene is here and as soon as he comes over this way, we will snag him for an interview. Earlier we caught up with Sheppard Granger and his lovely wife Carson Boyett Granger, who told us about the strides the Sheppard Granger Foundation for Troubled Teens have been making. We are looking forward to hearing more wonderful things about this organization in the future...*

Carson checked her watch and then glanced up at her husband. "It's not like Roland to be so late."

Sheppard nodded and took a sip of his punch. They were surrounded by his sons and their wives as well as Striker Jennings, Quasar Patterson and Stonewall Courson.

Also included were Shana and Jules' father, Ben Bradford and his wife Mona. The only person missing was Roland. "I'm sure he's on his way, sweetheart," he assured Carson. He knew she was right to be worried. Roland was seldom late for anything.

"I talked to him less than an hour ago," Striker offered. "He was leaving home then. Unless he made a pit stop somewhere, he should have been here by now."

Sheppard didn't say anything as he glanced over at the entrance. He hoped Roland walked through the door soon, or else Carson would continue to worry. Tonight was one for celebration since he planned to tell the world about the latest additions to the Granger family. Carson had had her first doctor's appointment, and according to the doctor, the soon-to-be-mother was doing fine. There shouldn't be any complications during this pregnancy.

Sheppard had been present during that doctor's visit and he doubted he'd ever forget how he'd felt when he heard the sound of their baby's heartbeat. Whenever he thought about the fact there would be three Granger babies born within weeks or days of each other, he was almost overwhelmed with joy.

"Who is that?" Stonewall asked, staring at a woman on the opposite side of the room.

Everyone's head turned, but it was Jules who spoke up. "Oh, that's Joy Ingram. *Detective* Joy Ingram."

Stonewall's head snapped around. "She's a cop?"

Jules smiled. "Yes, and a really good one. She transferred to the city a year and a half ago. You want an introduction?"

Before Stonewall could answer, Striker spoke up. "She's a cop, Jules. Stonewall doesn't do cops."

"I'll make an exception this time," Stonewall quickly countered. "Yes, Jules, please introduce us." It didn't take long before Detective Ingram was within range for Jules to snag her attention.

Sheppard who'd been quietly observing things unfold knew Stonewall well enough to know he was definitely attracted to the woman wearing the emerald green dress. He wondered if Stonewall even realized he was still holding the woman's hand as introductions were being made.

Sheppard was finding the entire scene amusing. This was the first time he'd ever known Stonewall to be taken with any woman, and the fact that she was a cop definitely made things interesting. It was a known fact that Stonewall didn't particularly like cops. But Shep would admit the woman was beautiful. Umm, he wondered...

Carson opened her purse and checked her phone. If Roland was running late, she hoped he would have texted her to let her know why. She breathed a sigh of relief when she saw his number appear on her phone. "I got a missed call from Roland," she said to everyone. She then excused herself from the group to stand in a quieter area to call him back.

Sheppard had been laughing at something Ben had said when he happened to glance over to Carson. The look on her face immediately alerted him that something was very wrong. He was about to go to her when she hurried back to the group. Obvious signs of panic were on her face.

"Carson? Sweetheart? What's wrong?" he asked, reaching out for her when it looked as if she would pass out.

His words got everyone's attention. They turned to glance over at Carson who looked quite upset about something. "Someone used Roland's phone to call me from the hospital."

"The hospital?" Sheppard asked, not understanding.

Carson nodded. "Yes. Someone tried hijacking Roland's car on his way here tonight. He's been shot."

"Shot!" A chorus of voices said in disbelief.

"Yes." Carson took a deep breath, trying hard to pull herself together. "We need to get to the hospital, Sheppard. They had to rush Roland into surgery and the person I talked to said it didn't look good."

"Let's go." Taking his wife's hand, Sheppard quickly ushered her toward the exit doors. It was going to be a long night....

THE PLOT THICKENS IN THE PROTECTOR SERIES
Book 1 – Striker Jennings' story titled
FORGED IN DESIRE

Coming January 31, 2017
Click here to preorder book:
From Amazon - http://amzn.to/2f9OgKI
From Barnes and Nobles - http://bit.ly/2fxMVub

Turn the page for a sneak peek at Forged in Desire (Book 1 of the Protector Series, Striker Jennings' story)

THE GRANGER SERIES CONTINUES WITH THE PROTECTOR SERIES

By Brenda Jackson

**

Margo head jerked up. "What?! You hired him without consulting me?"

"I saw no need. He came highly recommended, Margo. I understand he's good at what he does and that's what I want."

That wasn't what she wanted. She wanted to vet her own bodyguard. The last thing she needed was someone breathing down her neck, watching her every move and telling her what she could and could not do, which is exactly what the sort of man her uncle hired would do.

"And I hope you follow his orders, Margo. His job is to keep you alive."

She scowled at him. "Since he came so highly recommended, I'm sure that he will."

Margo drew in a deep breath. She hated being a smart mouth; however, the thought of another man crowding her space for any reason—even to keep her alive—didn't sit well with her. She and Scott had lived in separate apartments and had tossed around the idea of moving in together. He was more for it then she was. During the weekends he had stayed over at her place, she'd been more than ready for him to leave on Monday morning. He never picked up after himself and depended on her to do practically everything. She'd begun to feel like his personal assistant rather than his lover.

She leaned back against the sofa. Her uncle moved from the window to take the chair across from her. "So what do you know about this person whose presence I have to put up with for no telling how long?" she asked. "Who recommended him, Uncle Frazier?"

There was a long pause. Hadn't her uncle heard her question? Just in case, she repeated it.

"Someone I know."

"So this person has used him before?"

"Not sure."

She lifted a brow. "Yet you've taken his word for it?" She could tell her questions were agitating him. She was ready to dig deeper when the doorbell rang.

"I hope that's him," her uncle said, standing quickly.

She stood as well. A part of her hoped it wasn't him. Why did she feel certain her life would be changing? Probably because it would. A madman was on the loose. A killer for hire. Did Murphy Erickson really think he would be set free from prison? If nothing else, these additional deaths were on his hands. Had the man forgotten that Virginia was a death-penalty state? Did he care?

Margo moved toward the door, her uncle right on her heels. She started to say something and decided not to waste her time. What was the point? Her uncle had arranged for her to have a bodyguard regardless of whether she wanted one or not.

Upon reaching the door, she turned to her uncle. "Like I said, I won't have him underfoot, Uncle Frazier."

"If it means keeping you alive, I don't care if he's underarm," he responded tersely.

She rolled her eyes before turning back to the door. "Who is it?"

"Striker Jennings."

Striker? What kind of name was that?

She turned to her uncle, who nodded and said, "That's him."

She wanted to see what kind of guy went by the name *Striker*. She stared through the peephole and, as if he knew what she was doing, he looked directly at her. The moment their gazes connected, something—she wasn't sure what—made her breath catch.

Her uncle heard it and quickly asked, "What's wrong?"

Margo drew in a deep breath as she pulled away. "Nothing." She was lying. Who was this man? Why did just staring into his eyes have such an effect on her? The thought that he would be sharing her space...for who knows how long...was rather unsettling.

"Well, aren't you going to let him in?"

Instead of answering her uncle's question, she opened the door. And there he stood. The man named Striker Jennings. Instead of focusing on his eyes like before, she took in the entire man. And what a man he was. He was tall, way over six feet. And he was big. Muscular in a dark business suit and looking totally professional and serious. Why was her gaze intrigued by his broad shoulders, bulging biceps and flat abs? And those heavily lashed, dark eyes, the same ones she had stared into just moments ago, seemed to say, "Go ahead and try me."

Try him? Margo swallowed deeply while thinking, How? With what? And for how long? She snapped back to her senses when her uncle came around to verify the man's identity and said, "Show me credentials."

Although the man gave her uncle a look that all but told him what he could do with the credentials he'd asked for, the man shifted his duffel bag into the other hand before pulling an identification card from his jacket pocket. She and her uncle looked at it. *Lamar Jennings.* So Striker wasn't his real name. And he worked for a Summers Security Firm. There was a nice picture of him, but the real thing standing in front of her was so much better. Almost too much. Far too pleasing on any woman's eyes. His nutmeg-colored facial features were way too mesmerizing. Way too captivating to even be considered merely handsome. Definitely riveting. She noted there was nothing soft about him and detected a hardness that would kick ass first and ask questions later.

Her uncle handed the ID card back to him. "Come on in, Jennings."

"Striker," he corrected, not moving an inch. It was as if he needed to establish a few things up front and what he wanted to be called was one of them.

Her uncle didn't say anything, and she wondered if he would. Although he often accused her of being stubborn, Frazier Connelly could be just as stubborn. Even more so. The two men stared hard at each other and then, as if her uncle had decided it would be in his best interest to be the one to concede, he said, "Okay. Come in, *Striker.*"

She stepped aside when he walked past her and she closed the door behind him.

"You come highly recommended," her uncle was saying, extending his hand out to the man.

"Do I?" Striker replied, accepting her uncle's handshake.

"Yes, and this is my niece, Margo Connelly. The woman I'm depending on you to keep safe."

He turned his dark, penetrating eyes on her. She could feel a deep stirring in the pit of her stomach when he extended his hand out to her. "Ms. Connelly."

Margo accepted his hand and suddenly an intense rush of desire tore into her. It took everything she had not to snatch her hand back. She'd never met this man before. Didn't know a thing about him other than that he'd been hired by her uncle. Yet she was attracted to him. She'd heard of sudden attraction but had never been the recipient of it, until now.

Even though he was impeccably dressed in a business suit, she detected a rough edge. And she suspected if the need arose, he could be lethal. As far as she was concerned, lethal and good-looking was one hell of a combination. She *was* a woman and there was nothing wrong with appreciating a well-muscled, nicely built man when she saw one.

"Mr. Jennings," she said, pulling her hand from his.

"Striker," he corrected.

Instead of acknowledging his correction, Margo didn't say anything, not sure she could find her voice even if she'd wanted to. At that moment a semblance of heated desire fanned low in her stomach. On top of that, her mind was still reeling from the sensations caused from their handshake. She felt irritated wondering what in the world was going on here. Putting the *appreciation* thing aside, it was totally unlike her to be *this* affected by any man. Although she relished eye-candy like any other female might, she'd never let a man bring out the lustful side of her. In fact, to be totally honest, she hadn't been aware she had one until now. She hadn't been involved with a man since Scott. And that had been her choice. Her passion was her work and it superseded any intimate feminine needs. She'd learned not to place any man at the top of her pedestal.

That decision had come about after her last two serious relationships had left a bad taste in her mouth. Her attitude was that she didn't need a man to be happy since all they seemed to do was disappoint her anyway. She liked her life just the way it was. Uninvolved, unattached and drama-free. At least it had been drama-free before the Erickson trial.

As Margo continued to study the man who'd entered her home, she had a feeling she was in a heap of trouble that had nothing to do with any assassin's attempt on her life.

WELCOME TO THE EXCITING READING WORLD OF
NEW YORK TIMES AND USA TODAY BEST SELLING AUTHOR
BRENDA JACKSON

Get Your Free Brenda Jackson App

Available for iPhone, iPad and Android. Scan the QR Code with your smartphone, or search Brenda Jackson in your app store!

Want to receive Brenda Jackson's monthly newsletter? Click here!

http://www.brendajackson.net/?page_id=57

Visit Brenda's website at –
www.brendajackson.net

BRENDA JACKSON BOOKS

There are over 10 million Brenda Jackson books in print.
Click here for a printable book list of all Brenda
Jackson books, the breakdown of the books in their
respective series and the order of books.

http://www.brendajackson.net/?page_id=10

Visit my website at – www.brendajackson.net

Download my FREE Brenda Jackson APP on your smart
phone!

The Grangers and Protector Series

The Granger Series
Book 1

The Granger Series
Book 2

The Granger Series
Book 3

The Granger Series
Book 4
December 2016
"Prequel To Book 1 of The Protector Series"

The Protector Series
Book 1
February 1, 2017